HARD 3

This is a work of fiction. Names, characters, businesses, places, events and incidents are either the products of the author's imagination or used in a fictitious manner. Any resemblance to actual persons, living or dead, or actual events is purely coincidental.

Published by ELITE PENS PUBLICATIONS

Written by: ANJELA DAY

HARD 3

Anjela Day

Prologue

Sacario

Looking into Ali's eyes I knew that shit had just gotten real. He stood beside me with the look of hurt in his facial expression and all I could do is accept what was coming. We all knew that one day this fuckin game would catch up to us; I just didn't think it would be my own brother slapping cuffs on my arms. I looked to my wife, tears flooded her face and it was nothing that I could do to stop them, I had failed Nya once again.

"Sacario Lamar Alton you are under arrest for the murder of Andrea Scott, and three counts of trafficking, a control substance do you understand?" Ali says and I nod my head yes.

"Cari," Nya cried and I didn't want to look at her. My brother handed me off to another officer and I shook my head as I walked out of the bedroom.

"Cari, Sacario baby no." My wife screams and it kills me, but in that moment I knew what I had to do. Lanya had been through enough, she didn't deserve waiting on my ass to get out of jail, "Fuck," I thought out loud. It's a million and one charges that I could have been charged with, but once again they trying to get me for something I had nothing to—Yeah I would be lying if I say I had nothing to do with that bitches death, call it tying up loose ends but this shit was never supposed to be traced back to me. When I made sure Dom bitch ass found out where Nya's mom was I sent that nigga Saint to do the job right and to make sure my son went unharmed. I never thought that my wife would take it so hard, but what the fuck could I do, it was done and over with. Shit, my only question was who the fuck leaked that I was behind the whole thing, and if Nya find out that I killed her mother and father can we ever get back right? I shake that thought and just knew that I needed to let my wife go she deserves better.

The excited officer forces me into the back of a squad car and it finally hits me, I'm going to jail...

Lanya.

I stood shivering and not because I was completely naked, but because I watched my whole world get flipped upside down. They had come in my home and ripped my husband from my arms. Accused him of doing what I knew he would never do and the worst part was the person that stood there and did nothing. His own fuckin brother was a fuckin rat. They dragged Sacario out of the room and all I could do was look at Ali like he was the fuckin devil himself. I snatched away from the two clowns holding me, and one put a gun to my head. I froze and looked up at Lee. He nodded his head and the man lowered his gun and that pissed me off ten times more. I sucked my teeth and rolled my eyes at Ali he looked my body over and rubbed his chin. "THIS CAN'T BE HAPPENIN'!" I scream out loud ripping the sheets off the bed and walking towards my closet where there were five cops tossing my belongings everywhere.

"The fuck are you doing?" I scream, Ali grabs my arm and I pull away cutting my eyes at him this was truly an; if looks could kill moment. I shake my head and walked out the I see police officers standing outside of my daughter's door like they're gone stop me from getting to her. I pause and turn in Deuce's room. An a officer is going through his things and I shot him a look and he walks out. I bent down and kiss my baby. As I stood he grabbed my neck, "mommy I love you." He said and I kiss him again laying him back down. Ali walks in the room and I want to kill his ass. I motioned to the door for him to leave no other words needed to be said. to the door I

5

gathered my thoughts and followed behind him. I walk down to Lyssa's room and look at the cop that is standing over her. Ali nods his big ass head and once again they take heave and vanish. 'This bastard!' I think to myself.

"Why are you following me?" I ask Lee he tossed a pair of jogging pants and a tank top at me.

"get dressed." He ordered I roll my eyes and laid Lyssa down to step into the oversize pants. I slipped into the shirt and looked back up at Ali.

"These are Cari's," I tell him. Standing with my hands crossed over my chest.

"Nya I didn't want –" I held my hand up not wanting to hear shit he had to say.

"YOU A FUCKIN RAT! I hope Nero kills you!" I place my index finger to his temple and said, "Pow!" He grabbed my finger and twisted my wrist until he had my entire body contorted in pain. I could barely breath I gasped for air, as he rested my body on his. I tried pulling away it was no use he grabbed my other wrist rendering me motionless.

"Stop it, calm the fuck down." He said through gritted teeth I want to fight, but I give up as I began to cry. He bent down I heard him breathing in my ear. I feel his body against mine I try to stay mad, but he is calming me. He kisses my ear and I feel a shock my nipples stiffen, I try pulling away but he holds me tighter. A minute passes and he slowly turns me to look at him.

Ali

My heart is racing just looking in this woman's eyes. I thought that I had gotten over the small attraction I had for her. However I was fooling myself, that was nothing small, I was in love with my brother's wife, t in that moment I wanted her..."Nya calm yo fuckin self! My brothers know who and what the fuck I am." She pulls back again and I grab her and slam her into the wall. I lift her chin to make sure she is looking at me. She starts to cry and I can't resist, I bend down and place my lips on hers. She kisses me back and her body moves into mine, I release her hands pulling her closer. I run my hands through her hair and she looks into my eyes as we pull apart. Lanya's lips parted and before I could think she raised her hand to smack me but I catch her hand and then feel a sharp pain between my legs. I grab my dick and want to kill her. "Fuck is—?"

"You a jealous piece of shit, I wouldn't be shocked if you set this shit up and framed him. Sad that you are in love with your brother's wife, loyalty nigga... have you heard of it!?" She says as I gasp for air she picks the baby up and I watch as she walks out the room. It took a minute to regain myself and just as I start to walkout the babies bedroom my phone rings I look at Dinero's number and know that I got to hear his fuckin mouth.

Dinero

The sound of my phone ringing for the third time bout damn near blows my high and pulls me out my bitch's pussy!" I reach over to the night stand and grab my phone. Kym sucks her teeth and I hit her with that look. She looks away and I answer the phone for my baby sister.

"Hell...,"

"Nero!?" Nya shouts before I get a chance to even say hello. "Please tell me that this is a bad ass dream. You couldn't have know Ali's bitch ass was a fuckin cop?" I pause as I look at the phone, 'SHIT!' I think out loud because if she know's then some shit just went down.

"Yeah I knew," I hear the wind blowing through the phone as Lanya says nothing.

"Nya, sis!?" I call out and I hear her suck her teeth.

"Fuck you O, how could you; of all people keep that shit from me!?" I look at the phone wanting to cut into her, but right now was not the time. "What happened Nya!?" I asked in a relaxed tone.

"That scum muthafucka bust in my bed room and dragged my man out in his fuckin basketball shorts! He didn't even let him fuckin get dressed Nero! He didn't even let him—," she started to cry and I stood to my feet.

"Man stay there, I'm on my way!"

"No don't come to me find my husband and make this right!" I suck my teeth and walk into my closet, tossed on a pair of jeans, and Timbs. No time for getting fly, I grab my wife beater off the bed, my keys from the dresser and walk out the door. 'Fuck,' I think to myself dialing Ali.

"Fuck happened?" I say before the nigga can utter a word.

"Shit, my hands are tied. Apparently that nigga Dom left. Files saying that nigga killed his girl's mom and they're running wit it! They hit some hoe he was fuckin wit house, 12 kilos and bitch sung like a bird. All I could do was bring him in."

"Fuck you mean she sung, what she knows you talk to Saint?"

"Nigga I got the shit handled, but that Trafficking not going nowhere boy doing ten, he know it and so do I." Ali tell me and I wonder what the fuck I'm gone do for ten years without my baby brother? "Shit was our empire strong enough to hang on?"

"Yo his wife want me to go where he at so I'm calling his lawyer, the red bone bitch and I will meet you at the station."

"Nigga its nothing you can do till morning, they did this shit so he would have to spend the fuckin night, just call ole girl and sit tight! I got to go"! Ali tells me. I did just that, I hit the Olivia chick up walked back in my house, laid pipe to my bitch and woke up to the sound of another phone call. The phone call that would blow my mind.

"Yo Bro twenty years, parole in ten, attempted murder, he took a plea." I couldn't even reply, I just ended the call and closed my eyes.

Lanya

Lord I just can't. I am so sick of being in my damn feelings, but this brave face is not for me, my heart hurts and I long to be with and touch my husband. I can't believe it has been two months since my husband has been in prison, all because his family stabbed him in his back. Loyalty what the fuck, is that just a word because it sure wasn't the Alton family. "Hands out!" A man says pulling me from my thoughts, I look up at the heavily armed man holding a hand held scanner in his hands and rolled my eyes as I step through yet another metal detector. My mind raced as I await this man to look me over. I was dressed in a black wrap around dress and a pair of Gucci heels. I stayed sharp, my husband had instilled that in me from day one. No one respects a bum, he told me. "All clear," the man says and I give him an innocent smile. The play cop admires my curves, so as I walk I give him a little extra too look at. I loved the extra attention.

I made sure to get there extra early so that I could avoid the traffic of these women bringing their children. I was kind of hurt because my husband had two children that he had not seen in quite some time. I couldn't help but fidget with my fingernails as I waited for what felt like an eternity. Finally a pretty, brown skin woman dressed as a play cop stepped out from behind what looked like a toll both. She held a clipboard in her hand and a huge smile on her face. She called out several names. I was nervous as I listened closely. "Alton, Sacarrio," she says misreading his name. I stood, gave myself a once over and as I walked towards her I noticed that another woman had also made her way over to her as well. Her body was slender, but very curvy. Her skin was the perfect shade of brown and her hair was wavy with blond and brown highlights. She was dressed in a well-tailored white business suit and a pair of limited Gucci heels. I knew those heels well, because Sacario had purchased me the same ones not too long ago. I couldn't help but give this woman my complete attention. She was stunning and in that second I felt so insecure. She slowly turned to look at me as I stood steps away from her. That's when it hit me, who she was. "Morning Lakeisha," she says with an icy smirk on her face. I parted my lips to speak, however my nerves wouldn't allow me. I nodded my head and raised my eyebrow. "Are you related?" The guard asked and I couldn't help, but laugh.

"No," Olivia says before I have a chance to.

"Well I'm sorry, I can only allow one woman back at a time." She looks us both over, and I want to scream. She went into the tan briefcase that I was sure cost a million dollars and pulled out a business card.

"I'm Mr. Alton's attorney." She looked at her clipboard and then she looked from myself, to Olivia. I felt as if she was waiting for me to identify myself.

"I'm his wife." I just handed her my ID that rested in my hand. I knew better than to bring my purse or anything that I would have to lock away in one of those ratty lockers. The guard looked us both over again and nodded so that we could both follow.

"Being that you da lawyer, and she his wife should ent be a problem." The woman said in the worst English I had ever heard in my life, and I was raised around hood people. She led us into an open room where there were cheap plastic chairs and even cheaper tables, which were nailed to the floor. I sat in one of the chairs while little miss perfect, stood. A group of men walked into the room and my body began to shake. I didn't know why I was so nervous, I just knew that I missed Cario and not even the bitch Olivia would steal the joy from me. I looked up at the men walking to their families and couldn't truly tell them apart, most of the men were either black or Mexican. Being that my husband could past for either, I was a bit lost until the last man walked in the room. He was tall and even with a full beard and jail overalls on, he had a swag no one could deny. His walk was as full of confidence as he was. I smiled as he walked closer. Tears

13

filled my eyes and my heart slowed. He licked his full lips and looked at the two of us, shook his head and sat down. Olivia walked over to the table, I couldn't miss the huge grin on her face if I was deaf, dumb or blind. She finally sat in one of the plastic chairs and crossed her legs seductively.

"What you doing here?" Sacario asked and I looked at Olivia with a devilish smile. I turned to Olivia with a raised eyebrow, awaiting her answer as well. However she didn't even acknowledge that he was speaking to her.

"Nya, why are you here?" He asks finally looking at me with those sexy eyes that I have longed to see.

"Excuse me?"

"Why are you here? I told you I didn't want you and the kids coming."

"So I didn't bring the kids, but I'm your fuckin wife!" I yelled. Every eye in the room appeared to have fallen on me. I cleared my throat and looked away so that he wouldn't see that I was starting to cry. Damn Sacario, for embarrassing me in front of this woman; belittling me as if I was some side bitch. I could feel both of them looking at me, so I stood up wiping my face with the back of my hand.

"Well Killa you want me to go?" His eyes were sad.

"Baby I just don't need you coming up in here. Seeing you is killing me," he stood up and walked over to me reaching for my hand. He pulled me into his arms and kissed my neck. "NO TOUCHING." Was yelled over the room but it was too late, Sacario had already gotten me worked up. I could feel my pussy juicing up. My heart was racing, and that small touch had my body at his mercy. I knew I had to shake off what I was feeling and get back to the right state of mind. I took my seat and looked at Olivia as she watched Cari's every move.

"So what am I supposed to do Cari?" I asked as he took his seat.

"The same thing you have been doing, sitting on yo ass or spending his money!" Olivia chimed in and my head snapped in her direction. I looked at the stare that Sacario was giving Olivia, but it wasn't good enough.

"Bitch, I have my own, my nigga taught me that so I don't have to spend shit of his." I stood to my feet ready to knock this bitch in her place. Sacario stood up trying to get me to calm down.

"Nya, this is not the time nor the damn place."

"No fuck you and her, I'm your wife!" I reminded him once again, looking at the guard that was now caressing his weapon. Tears flooded my eyes and I was not in the mood to wipe my face. "You know what, I'm not a fool and I see what's going on, but you don't have to throw it in my face. But trust Sacario, she will never look at you, nor love you the way I do."

"Fuck you talking about? She my lawyer."

"Yeah whatever, Killa."

"Watch yo mouth, yo tone and yo words Nya."

"FUCK YOU SACARIO!" I wiped my face with the back of my hand gave Olivia one last look and walked towards the exit. That was not supposed to happen.

≈≈≈≈≈≈

I couldn't wait till I got home. I was fuming, I was so grateful to have Kym and Dinero. They had the kids so I could be alone and do what I needed to do. I walked in my home and straight to my bedroom. My first thought was to get drunk and cry, but I was so hurt, all I could think of was what I should have said. I walked over to my dresser and pulled out a pen and pad. It was so much I wanted to say I didn't know if I could get the words out. I walked back over to my bed and flopped down. I stared at the paper, I was hurt and truly didn't know what I should say.

Dear Sacario,

When we met I was so dead inside. I was young, hurt and didn't know what was next in my life, you changed that. For that I will always feel in debt to you. However, you should never get it confused with the fact that through all that I fell in love with you, the first time you looked at me. I never thought that I was good enough to know you, let alone become your wife. You gave me that, I stood before you and promised to love and trust you no matter what. I have and continue to do so. You are my King, my heart, my soul. Without you I am living, but not alive. You are my husband and forever

I will fight for you, fight for us. Never ask me not to.

You may think that the people that come into our lives will

do right by you, but no woman can love you the way I

do. I hope that when you read this you will understand

why I reacted as I did. I am truly sorry.

I love you, Always and forever your wife

Lanya Alton.

Chapter 1 Alone

Behind every Powerful King is a QUEEN, and sometimes it takes a QUEEN to rule the KINGDOM... LONG LIVE THE QUEEN... Hard 3

Do you believe in love at first sight? Yeah neither did I. That was until I met Sacario Lamar Alton. He was superman minus the cape. Rocking Timbs and Gucci, he was by far the sexiest man I had ever met in my life. His body, swag and finesse alone were enough to make me want to be Mrs. Alton. I can't deny that the minute I sat beside him I wanted him to say hello. I knew I had a man, but never had I saw a man that took my breath away however, when our eyes met I was in love. My heart was racing from the inception. He had this quiet arrogance to him. He controlled the room without speaking a word, and when he did speak he gave me chills

It was easy for anyone to see that we did not fit together. A boss nigga with an insecure waitress, how does that work? I had no place in his life, so he became King and changed the rules. I thought that was by far one of the scariest times in my life. I thought that once Sacario and I had made it through the blackmail, the cheating, lies, rape and so much more, he and I could get through anything. What a fool was I to think that?

Normally it's these bitch ass females that flea when they find out there man has to do a bid. Not me, I intended to hold my man down, my vows were real to me. However, my husband didn't have the same plans for us. I don't know if he was mad at me for stepping to that Barbie Doll that he called a lawyer, or if he realized that he was on a whole nother level than I was, nonetheless it had been six months and I had not received a call from him. I was starting to feel as if the letters I sent on a daily were not reaching him. It had gotten to the point where I found myself crying religiously.

I sat up in my bed listening to Ashanti, with a glass of Patron in my hand. It was my second, and for some reason I knew it wouldn't be my last. The sound of the phone ringing pulled me from the pity party I was throwing in the bottom of my glass. I grabbed the phone and laid back down on my bed answering the call.

"This call is from a Federal Facility, press one to accept, two to decline and three to block caller." The recording said and I looked at the keypad on my phone tempted to press three. It was no doubt in my head that it was Sacario.

"Hello," I say pressing one."

"Fuck you doing?" I didn't respond, I just held the phone for a moment.

"Lanya you hear me?"

"Yes Sacario, I hear you!"

"So fuckin answer me! Where are my kids?"

"They're asleep," I said slurring my words just a bit.

"You sound high or some shit, fuck wrong with you?"

"Me Sacario, I have not heard from you since my visit, when you asked me why the hell I was there to see my fuckin husband! So what the fuck is you calling me for? I know you getting my fuckin letters, I know...

Damn it Sacario, just say you don't want me anymore save us both the fuckin heart ache." I could hear him breathing harder, he cleared his throat.

"Olivia needs to drop some papers off to you tomorrow, will you be there?"

"Why is she coming to our home, I don't want that bitch here Cario, I don't want your bitch in my home!"

"Lanya what the hell is you talking about? You sitting there bitching and crying over a bitch I'm not looking at while I'm locked the fuck down. That's that insecure shit that you need to grow the fuck up out of, damn. You too old for that shit. That's my fuckin lawyer and she will be there in the morning, make yourself available." Sacario said ending the call and leaving me with tears in my eyes.

My husband had me fucked up. I stood to my feet, walked over to the dresser and poured myself one more glass of the strong tonic when the phone rang again. It was so loud I damn near dropped my glass. Taking a deep breath I walk over to the bed and answered the phone.

"Yes?" I say to the unregistered number.

"May I speak to Sacario please?" A woman says and I get a gut feeling this is bad. Flopping down on my bed I down the rest of my drink.

"He's not here however this is his wife, may I help you?" The woman sighed and held the phone breathing like a stalker.

"Look I don't have time to play, is it something I can help you with?"

"I need to speak to him, it's really important!"

"Sorry to inform you honey, he won't be getting back with you so clearly I'm yo best bet, so speak your mind or get off my damn phone!" I pulled the phone away from my ear and I heard her yell "HELLO?"

"Yes?"

"Can we meet somewhere?"

"I don't even know who I'm talking to."

"My name is Nikki, I use to work for—."

"You use to work at the bar," I say cutting her off.

"Yeah, how did you know?"

"What do you need with my damn husband?" Now I was pissed off, this bitch really had the nerve to be calling my husband. It was bad enough that I walked in on their escapade, but now I had to talk to her on the phone. I thought when I gave that bitch 50 stacks to leave I would never hear her voice again, now here it is almost 8 years later and she on my phone. How the fuck did she even get my house number? I sucked my teeth as she pled her case for me to meet her. I knew I had been drinking and it was a bad idea, however I would have kicked myself if I didn't go. What's that saying curiosity killed the cat, well for some reason I could smell death!?

≈ ≈ ≈ ≈ ≈

I walked into Coney Island, where Nikki and I had agreed to meet. I was so grateful that Kym was there to sit with the kids. I was really nervous and truthfully wanted her with me, but I couldn't tell her that I was meeting with one of Cario's whores. Who probably wanted another pay off. I caressed my purse and took a seat in one of the booths. I couldn't really recall what she looked like, I just knew that she was a pretty brown skin chick that had me questioning was I pretty enough. That was the past and I needed to get over it. I looked down at my ringing phone, then up at the door to see a woman with a small child walk in. I placed my phone in my purse and sat up as the woman looked at me, but seemed unsure if I was the right person.

"Your Sacario's wife?" She questioned with a smirk on her face.

"Yes and if you don't mind I want to get straight to it." She sat down and sat the small child beside her.

"Why are you calling my husband? I gave you fifty thousand dollars to leave my family alone."

"Yeah that was until I found out I was pregnant."

"So what the fuck that got to do with Sacario?"

"He's the father." This bitch looked dumb, my man had been locked up for almost a year and now she saying that she has a child with him. I looked at her perfectly fit body and rolled my eyes.

"So where is the baby?" I ask going into my purse, I figured she really just wanted more cash and at this point I would have paid anything to get my sanity.

"This is him, this is Jayson Lamar." Jayson Lamar I said to myself, wondering how she knew so much about Sacario. I guess she was more than just sex. That shit was starting to cut like a knife to the heart. I looked at the child and he looked to be the same age as Deuce. "How old is he?" She smiled and rested the child's head on her arm. "He's seven." I was beyond pissed looking at this bitch I had paid to go away but all she did was go away and have a child. A child that was only months younger than my son. A son that I wasn't even sure belong to Sacario.

I mean I had only been with one other man when Sacario and I made love that night, but Keith had drummed it in my head that my son was his, I always questioned if I was pregnant already when I made love to Cario.

The little boy raised his head and he had the same eyes my son had, they were brown, the color of honey just like every Alton man. I looked for features that could distinguise this boy, from Sacario; however I found none. Jayson looked just liked Deuce, and that alone was crazy. I had convinced myself that Deuce belonged to Keith. I told myself the nigh Sacario and I made love that I was already pregnant with Deuce. Now I was questioning everything, but that this child was Sacario. He was my husband's double, also the spitting image of Deuce. This encounter was leaving me more lost than when I first stepped in the restaurant.

"So what do you want Nikki?" She rolled her eyes and looked at me like I was annoying her but that bitch knew what she was doing, 50 stacks was more than enough to kill that kid. But she wanted Sacario's child; truthfully I couldn't blame her

"I want your husband to be a man and take care of his son!" She yelled standing from the table.

"I'm sure he gladly would if he wasn't in jail for the next twenty years Nikki, so I'm all you got. if you want me to play step mommy, fine I will but as for Sacario being a great daddy, I don't see that happening with him behind bars."

"My mother was right," she said and I leaned in her face.

"How so?"

"She said his bitch ass would try and get out of it but that's fine, I have a new man and he is way more gangsta then yo bitch ass nigga. Trust Jay is not gone to let Sacario play Jayson to the side; so tell that nigga get ready for war."

"War bitch Cario is locked up!?"

"All the better that means that his bitch ass won't see the bullet coming." Nikki was no longer just a waitress, she had come into her own; I wasn't impressed.

"Fuck you threating my husband for?"

"It's not a threat, it's a promise, Sacario thought he could get you to flash cash and I would go away."

I laughed; hell if Cario knew I was here he would have a heart attack. I thought to myself.

"First off bitch let's get this shit real clear. Sacario is more of a man than you will ever have, and as I stated my husband is in jail. You called at 10 pm which means he has no clue I'm here, so if you wanna do this shit the right way allow me to hold my husband's end up, I will gladly do so! Otherwise, I wish you and your child the best of luck." She sucked her teeth at me but I didn't care this bitch could try all she wanted, Sacario was my husband and I was going to do what I needed to hold him down.

"You are such a liar but whatever, keep Sacario ass, just tell him that he should be ready for the war coming his way." She stood grabbing her son and pulling him from the booth.

Her words stressed me but not for too long, I knew that Dinero and Ali would be prepared for whatever was to come their way. However I now questioned what role I would play in this family, where did I now fit?

Going home I laid in my king size bed, Mary J Blige's 'I'm Going Down' on repeat. I felt more alone and betrayed than I had in the eight years Sacario and I had been together. It left me wondering, what else could go wrong, what else did I not know about my husband's life? Gees did I not deserve happiness? Maybe not, maybe I was paying for the wrong I watched and had done nothing; maybe this was my sick Karma. I closed my eyes and wanted to pray for death, instead I prayed that I could hold up strong against whatever was going to come my way.

"Nya, Nya baby!" I hear and my heart damn near stops. I was afraid to open my eyes because it has to be my mind playing jokes. I could feel his soft touch run down my body and I shivered. I had to be losing it, Sacario was sentenced to twenty years, so who was in my bed sending chills down my spine and causing my pussy to throb. It had only been a few months I wouldn't dare cheat on Sacario. I forced my eyes open moving away from the strong hands that were now holding me firmly.

"Baby where you going? You didn't miss yo man?" Cario says and I damn near lose my mind.

"How, why, when oh my God, not why but...." I rolled into his arms and rested my lips on my husband. Never had anything felt so good. I had to pull myself away just to make sure he was truly there.

"Yeah baby it's me," he says spreading my legs, pulling my panties off and dropping to his knees to taste my juices. My pussy was plenty wet and the faster his tongue moved, the wetter I got and the harder it was for me to breathe. "Yes daddy! God!" I screamed releasing pent up frustrations that I had held onto for months. Sacario worked his hands up my body lifting my night-shirt, placing his lips on mine, my juices still covered them. I couldn't wait to feel his pipe inside of me. God it felt like it had been ages since I felt his stiffness. His thick wood was the only thing that could bring me to my knees and bring a smile to my face all in the same moment.

You can't tell me that God is not real. My prayers had been answered; my husband was lying in the same bed I had cried a hundred nights in. I didn't want to get up, but I had to check on our children. I sat up kissing my husband crawling over his sexy body. Taking one last look, I grabbed my robe and exited our bedroom. I made my way to Alyssa's bedroom to see Deuce rocking her.

"Hey momma's big boy," I say kissing his cheek. He smiled and lifted his shoulder to his face wiping away the kiss I had just planted.

"Whatever little boy," I said taking the baby from his arms and kissing her. She was dry and from the sound of the burp, she had been fed.

"You did all this Deuce?" I asked my son with a delighted mommy smile on my face. In a proud tone Deuce said "yes!" His chest stuck out and a smile covered his face, for the first time in a very long time I felt so good.

Chapter 2: Legacy

Lanya

It had been two months and I was feeling like maybe I had my life back. Despite how upset I was with Ali, that nigga had pulled it off. He and the bitch Olivia worked magic and brought Cario back home to me, yeah I knew it was still a chance he could go back. Although I had faith, Ali said that things looked good and because of that I had to remain strong. However, Sacario still hadn't slowed the fuck down.

I won't lie, I wished he would stay home. I feared that if he did, I wouldn't be unable to look him in the face. I still had not told him about Nikki's visit, the child she claimed was his and of course the threats that she had promised her so called man would deliver.

"Hey baby," Sacario says walking into our bedroom looking like a million bucks in just a simple pair of True Religion jeans, a Ed Hardy T-shirt and Timberlands on his feet but God the way everything fit him to perfection, always turned me on. I stood walking behind him, wrapping my hands around his waist and resting my head on his back.

"Sup sexy?" He says pulling me in front of him placing a kiss on my lips.

"Um you, I missed you." I whined standing on my tippy toes kissing his neck.

"Can you prove that?" He said kissing my lips sweetly.

"I sure can," I say running my hands up his shirt, felling his well-toned stomach.

"Damn ma, don't start shit you not gone finish," Sacario warns, lifting me off my feet. A smile present on my face when Ali walked in our bedroom. I still had not forgiven him from his last visit, and here he was stopping our flow once again.

"Nigga you forget I was down stairs?" Lee says handing me a letter and leaning against the wall like he was going to watch us. I ripped the letter open, still looking atat Ali with daggers in my eyes.

"Who the fuck writing yo ass from jail?" Sacario says snatching the envelope as it hits the bed. I shrug my shoulders and continue to read the letter, I can feel Sacario's eyes on me and I give him a fake smile. Tears fill my eyes but I know if they fall, Sacario would read the letter and yet another thing from my past would be revealed.

"Who is it from babe?" Cario asked and I smile again.

"Yo nigga, I love that you got twenty people on the way,and yo ass in yo wife's face." Lee says and I bring my eyes from the letter. "What's going on?"

"Yeah babe, no big deal, that's why I'm back so early. I need you to order some food, I'm having a few people over in about two hours." Sacario says like what he is asking of me is a simple task. I roll my eyes as a silent protest.

"Sacario what kind of people? You know it takes weeks to plan a get together."

"You don't have that long so just order some shit. My business partners are flying in."

"God Sacario really? God!" Sacario cut his eyes at me, smacking my ass when I standing up almost forgetting the letter. I grab the letter from the bed, pull my hair over my shoulder and braid it. I pick up my phone from the dresser and skim through it. I call a few places that I use when I didn't feel like cooking. I didn't want anything over done, this was my husband's crowd and most of them were a bit snobby. "God Cario, I have to go buy all new glasses because it's too late to order glasses and dishes." He flashes his perfect white teeth and I melt, grabbing my purse and keys, slipping on some gym shoes and walking out of the bedroom.

Sacario

'Suga sharp,' is what the old pimps use to say, and I can't deny that is how I was looking. I had Gucci's on my feet and Armani on my body, it got no better and white was my color. No matter how hard anyone tried, niggas had nothing on me.

I was relieved that Olivia had worked her magic and got me out, but now she had become too clingy, wanting to be a part of my organization. I would be a fool to deny her, but shit, not even my wife was allowed to know it all. This is why, despite the fact that I had decided to let Liv into my shit, she would not be at the roundtable. My roundtable was a table of true Boss niggas. And although there was no head of the table I was the supplier to them all, so of course they all knew who was really running things.

My wife worked her ass off in those two hours and had everything up and running, include the fact that she was dressed in a white dress that showed just enough body. I walked downstairs to see her greeting the guest, as most were already there standing around talking amongst each other.

"Hey babe, let me know when everyone is here," I tell my wife kissing her face and grabbing a glass of champagne from one of the trays posted all over the room. I raise my eyes when my right hand walks through the door, my nigga Saint had been a loyal member of our family since he was like ten years old. When he was a kid we called that nigga Sure Shot, because it wasn't a target he couldn't take out, nor a gun he couldn't use. However, recently Lee had started calling him The Saint. Not only did this nigga bless the pistol, the nigga was a stone cold assassin. He could kill a man with his bare hands and sit next to you like he had done nothing. the name was coined because Saint sent niggas to meet Jesus period. He was a cold blooded killer that I rarely caught in a weak moment. However, lately he had been seeing a new chick that had his nose wide open. I wanted to look down on him, but it was a feeling I knew to well.

"What up Boss? I checked all the exits, the gates are locked and I think that everyone is here." Saint says and I nod my head although Saint's eyes are no longer on me. He has a smirk on his face and he rubs his hands together like a starving man.

"Baby I think that's everyone." Lanya says running her hands over my stomach. I kiss her face and tap her ass when she walks away. Saint's eyes full of lust follow my wife. Saint looks to the ground as I turn my head to look at him. The normal man I would kill just for the thoughts that filled that niggas head, however Saint was different. I didn't stress the fact that he could kill me in one shot because I didn't get the name Killa from being a weak nigga. Saint was different because he was the son of Samuel Silk Marks, and his side bitch. Yeah he was my wife's baby brother and neither had a clue.

"No disrespect boss to you or your wife, it's just something special about her." He told me and I laughed. I nodded my head in agreement and made my way into the office where everyone had begun to gather.

Chapter 3: The Conglomerate

Sacario

I stood before eighteen men that ran some of the biggest cities and states. In this crowd that included; Geovanni from the Bronx, Ricardo from Texas, and of course the Marks from flint, Boris the Russian from Chicago and across from him was Dontay Lawton, the mayor of Chicago. I stood before all of them, this is what made me king. All these men were gathered because of me. Ali was to my right, Dinero to my left. We watched as everyone took their seats before I stood and took the floor.

"The reason I stand before you is because several of us are facing court cases. In no way can this be a mere coincidence. It has been brought to my attention that there is quite a few holes in everyone's camp, including my own."

"The only hole is the rat sitting beside you. I refuse to discuss anything knowing that it's a fuckin FED in the fuckin room." Smooth Marks says and I smile knowing he's referring to my brother.

"Nigga I kill for less," I tell that nigga looking back at my brother sitting straight up in his chair.

"You not half the man your father was," Dice Marks says and I laugh.

"Only his killers would know."

"That pussy nigga blew his brains out, he couldn't deal with the fact that my brother was better at business than he was." Smooth says causing me to draw my gun. Before I knew it, I was looking at the business end of over fifteen guns.

"Saint grab them gun's up," I ordered. Wondering why that shit wasn't done upon entrance. I hand Saint my gun and watch as he collect the other guns. The Russian Boris, refused to release his gun and before he could blink, Saint had a bullet in his ear.

"Anyone else have a problem with the no gun rule that I just instated?" I asked watching every man place their weapon into the box Saint was now carrying around.

Saint gathered the guns and stood in the back of the room. I looked down at Boris as his brains leaked onto the table, and shook my head.

"As I was saying," I paused to look at the Marks brothers.

"I'm sure that the inside man is someone trusted by all parties, or someone close. This person knows more than their fair share of information and can bring most of us to our knees. I'm not your father so I'm not here to tell you how things should be done, just that my family will no longer deal with anyone outside of this room. I am sure that by cutting out the middle man things will run smoother and we will have less lawyer and court fees." I went on to tell the men my plans on a brighter future.

Chapter 4 Reckoning

Dinero

The loud had me lifted, but not as high as I would have liked to be. I choked from the smoke and passed the blunt to Lee. He was stressing over the fact that since people knew he was a cop, that he would have no respect in the game. I assured him that was insane but the truth was I knew that now he was outed, he risked getting locked the fuck up because of some rat trying to cut a deal.

"Yo nigga maybe you should take a step back. I mean shit going down it's yo ass on the line," I tell him and he sucks his teeth looking away. I take the blunt from his hands and take a pull.

"My nigga you sound like a bitch. If I fuckin go down, I just go down. We blood and I'll be damned if a fuckin badge will change that. Shit I fuckin got this badge to protect us, now you asking me to step the fuck away. Fuck you pussy." Lee says standing and starting towards the door. I lifted my glass from the table and chucked it at the door, it shattered and fell to the ground causing Lee to stop in his tracks.

"Nigga protect us?" I stood to my feet and rushed to stand eye to eye with him.

"Bitch I'm your big brother, I protect you!" I yell at that nigga, mad enough to go in on his head.

"What's going on?" Kym says rushing into my office.

"It ain't shit wrong, babe get a broom and clean this shit up." I tell Kym smacking her ass and pulling her in for a kiss.

After my brother left I showered and dressed for bed. Walking into my bed room I look at my girl sitting on the middle of the bed reading.I laid in the bed watching my girl, for the first time I realized how happy I was to have her. I pulled her down beside me kissing her neck.

"What bae?" She said rubbing my stomach.

"You gone give me a seed?" I ask her, catching her off guard and she rolls her eyes.

"What you rolling yo eyes for?" She walked away and started to straighten our bedroom.

"Kym you hear me?"

"Yeah I heard you O!"

"And you gone give me a seed?"

I asked sucking my teeth, pissed that this was something she had to think on.

"Why the fuck you act like I'm not talking to you?" I stand up pulling her body into mine. I plant kisses on her neck and rub her stomach.

"Nero, I don't want a baby right now."

"Fuck you mean, why the fuck not?" I asked releasing her body.

"I just don't want to act like Nya. She is so flaky and everyone kisses her ass but no one really wants to be around her. Oh and the weight gain, no I can't."

"Fuck you mean you can't, so we never gone have a fuckin seed? Kym that's some bull shit and you know it."

"O it's not yo body."

"Really Kym that's your defense!?" I look at my girl feeling like I judged her wrong. Feeling let down, that she is not the woman I will be spending my life with. I grab my keys, phone and wallet off the dresser, giving my girl an icy stare and exit.

"O," she yells and I continue out the door.

"Dinero you just gone walk out because we fight?" Kym runs out the front door yelling and I turn around ready to knock her the fuck out, but I stop.

"Do what you wanna do Kym, I don't have time for this."

"O can we please just talk about this?"

"Not shit to say Kym, you don't want to have my seed, the next bitch will." I told her hoping in to my truck and peeling out."

I pulled up at the bar beyond pissed off. It had been a minute since I found myself tossing shots of King Louie back as if I had no liver. "Bro you good?" Killa says sitting beside me, grabbing a shot glass from behind the bar and pouring himself a drink. I couldn't do anything but laugh while downing another shot.

"I talked to Lee, he told me you told him to take a few steps back."

" what you think, I'm wrong?"

"Nah, I agreed with you, so that nigga double pissed. What you thinking on?" Killa ask and I down my seventh shot.

"Yo nigga slow up," he said when this bomb bitch appears in front of me, rocking the tightest jeans and a shirt that's showing damn near her whole top half.

"Buy me a drink daddy," she says and I smile.

"Nah I can't, but you can buy me a drink!" I tell her, reaching and grabbing another shot glass from behind the counter. She smiles taking the seat beside me and grabs my shot. She downs the drink and smiles. That shit was sexy as hell and this bitch was about to get fucked. I hopped up and led the way to the office admiring her thick legs, smooth brown skin and what I was sure was horse hair, draped down to her ass. I took that bitch in the office and as soon as the door closed, her pants hit the floor. Mami was about no games. Her ass was arched in the air as her body was rested on my desk.

Man I had always been a one woman nigga, but my bitch was tripping and this hoe was here, so I was smashing. I smacked her ass, ran my fingers between her legs then brought my hand up to take a whiff. Pussy was on point and the juices were flowing so I ripped the desk drawer open and pulled a gold wrapped condom out and dressed my dick for action. Her moans were sexy as fuck. I slid in and stroked her pussy. She gripped my dick like a pro. I could feel her warm juices running down my dick as she slides off my pole, drop to her knees and slips my pipe in her mouth. I wanna rip the condom off to feel her tongue and hot mouth, when she stands to her feet running her hands up my stomach.

Her fingers feels cold on my belly, so I look down to see that she's holding my Glock. Before I could grab the gun under the desk I try and grab the gun she's holding, but it fires forcing me to the ground. She laughs standing over me and pulled the trigger again. I tried to move as the hot lead filled my flesh. Maybe it was all the liquor or it was the shock that had me numb to the pain. However the blood feels cold as it leaves my body. I drop to my kees reach under the desk and grab my nine. Her back is turnt to me, as she pulls her phone and calls some one.

"Job is done" She says ending the call, and turning around.

"Tell Boris hello" She says just as I pull the trigger and fall to the ground. I tried holding the holes but the other ones were leaking and the truth was my body was too weak and I wasn't even sure if I was moving or just telling myself I was. My head felt light and only thing I could think was damn, as my eyes fluttered to stay open. Finally I feel her body on top of mine and I can die knowing I took that bitch with me. Tell him yo self I think as my eyes closes everything fades to black.

Chapter 5: Take Em' too War

Sacario

Even over that loud ass music I knew a fuckin gun shot when I heard them. I had no time to blink, I pulled my gun from my waist band, and prceeded up the stairs.

My heart was heavy as I rushed in the office. I was ready to blast, but to see some bitch laid dead on top of my brother as he laid there still. Tossing the hoe to the side, I pull my brother in my arms trying to stop the bleeding. Pulling my phone out to call 911, the door flew open and as soon as I pressed send, Could my eyes be deciving me? I looked at Antonio one of my guards just as I felt hot lead in my chest. I reach under the desk, pull the gun out and fire twice as I hit the ground. My chest burns and everything turns black.

Ali

Won't lie, I was pissed that both my brothers was losing faith in me. Fuck we was supposed to be fam and they treating me like a disloyal nigga. I understood that they didn't want me to lose my badge but fuck, what good is having a shield if I can't protect my brothers. I found myself laying next to a bitch that I couldn't even recall her name, guess that's what 15 shots of 1800 will do to you. My phone had been ringing all night, but fuck it whoever it was could kill they self. I was sick of being the my brother's keppers . My house phone rang again, and my door bell began to ring. I grabbed the cordless phone and slipped into a pair of jogging pants.

"I'm coming," I said listening to the nigga pound on my door.

"Alright nigga, I'm fuckin coming." I say ripping the door open looking at Lanya. She is wearing a fitted dress and a pair of Jordan's, no coat and it had to be twenty degrees in Michigan.

"What the hell lil bit, what's wrong?"

I say allowing her to push her way in.

"Nya what is it?"

"Where were you? Hunh where the fuck were you, you were supposed to protect him. Both of them and you were nowhere in sight, I always knew that you were a fuckin rat bastard." She says and I grab her pressing her body against the wall.

"We have had this fuckin talk Lanya, watch ya words, slow down and say what you need to say." She wraps her arms around my body and places her face on my chest and starts to cry. My phone began to ring again, followed by the doorbell. Now I was worried. I walked to the door, Lanya still holding me tight, I open the door and answer the phone.

"What?" I say into the phone, looking at Saint shaking his head.

"It's a witness in Sacario case that just came forward. Some white girl Renae, she said she was engaged to him. We have a warrant for his arrest, do you want me to bring him in?" the caller says

"No I'll do it," I say feeling the weight of the world as I end the call and Saint shakes his head again.

"Nigga it's all bad, they both got sprayed."

"Who we talking bout?" I asked stupidly, looking down at Lanya cry. I damn near lose footing. What the hell was going on?

Lanya

I felt lost as hell, my heart felt like it was in a million pieces. I had survived from my husband getting shot, for him to wake up and lose it when they told him that it's a chance that Dinero won't make it. My husband and his brothers were close and I knew that losing one of them would send him into a fuckin killing spree. I walked into the hospital room he shared with Dinero, to see Kym balled up in a chair and Sacario, Ali, Saint and two others discussing something in a very low tone. I kiss Kym's cheek checking on her, however my eyes are roaming the room. I look at Saint and he looks the most serious of them all. Ali keeps looking at Sacario and nodding and I would kill to know what is being said, however I know that my place is where my husband places me.

"Hey bae," Cario says and I push my way through, bending to kiss his lips.

"Where the kids?" He ask and I smile.

"Well Deuce and Lyssa are with the nanny, but I still have this one with me." I place Sacario's hand on my belly and he draws back.

"The hell?"

49

"What's wrong baby?" I ask seeing his reaction.

"Fuck you mean what's wrong. How the fuck you get pregnant when I'm facing jail and my brother damn near breathing."

Unreal, I had rushed here to be by his side after leaving the doctor to tell him the news and he's mad at me, the fuck? I try to hold my tears but I'm pissed. I take two steps back to get myself together and Ali holds his pinky finger out. I grab it and hold tight and look at him and he winks. I feel a bit of relief when I hear tapping on the door and the sound of heels hitting the ground.

My eyes rise to meet Sacario's Barbie doll. Olivia walks in dressed to the T in a baby pink Chanel suit, Gucci pumps and here I stand in a pair of Seven jeans, Jordan's and an Ed Hardy T shirt. My hair in a sloppy bun. I was destroyed as she shot me an icy stare then bent to hug my husband.

"Sacario I just got in town when I heard! Oh my god how are you? How is your brother?" She ask looking to Dinero's bed. I just wanted to scream. Ali pulls my whole hand in his hands, tears were sitting in my eyes. I bit down on my bottom lip watching as every word the bitch said she felt she had to touch Sacario's shoulder.

"Are you comfortable?" She ask lifting Sacario's head and adjusting his pillow. Then leaning her breast into his face as she places the pillow back under his head and bends down to kiss his forehead. I take off to the sky going for that bitch dirty blonde hair. Saint grabs me before I get to her, and it takes Lee and Saint to hold me.

"Nya, Nya!" Kym yells finally speaking.

"Fuck is wrong with you? Don't you see my man is laying here and you acting stupid when yours is breathing?" Was she for real, I thought to myself, trying to regain my composure. I look at Lee then Saint and say, "I'm good." I start to walk away and finally Sacario speaks.

"Where you going now?" He ask with venom in his voice.

"To find some dick, clearly this bitch got yours." His eyes bucked and he sat straight up in his bed. "Repeat that shit!" He says looking from me to every man in the room.

"You heard me!" I said fear now present in my voice.

"Bitch I'll fuckin kill yo ass" he says pulling a gun from Saints waist band. He centers the gun on me and I stick my chest out trying not to show fear.

"Yo Killa chill," Lee said and Saint takes his gun from his hand and slips it back down his jeans. Olivia runs her hand over his chest to calm him and I am a lost, making my way out the door.

"Nya!" Lee calls out, but I refuse to answer"

"Man let her ass go; she a fuckin brat!" Sacario yells I turn to look at him. Hate filled my eyes and I spoke before I thought.

"Well Killa you a bitch, so we even!" I say walking out the room.

I made it to the elevator, pushed the down button and leaned against the wall. I guess I had lost it, because tears flooded my face. I lost my footing and slid down the wall. I felt a hand pulling me up, Saint stood over me and pulled me in his arms. He looked in my eyes, but didn't say a word to me. I could feel that it was something between us. He was cute, but not sexy. He had this soft look to him like Deuce. I smiled at the fact that this hard nigga that didn't smile at anyone, hell every time I saw Saint he was standing stiff like a sniper ready to take a shot. He bent to look directly in my eyes, licked his full lips and moved in for a kiss. I turned my head and quickly moved from his grasp.

"Man," Saint said looking embarrassed. He took a step back, ran his hands over his head walking away leaving me still a mess.

"Man everybody wants Nya!" A voice says and I roll my eyes and look up at Ali. He presses both hands on the wall cornering me in and he stares in my eyes like he is searching for my soul. At this moment he could have had it, I felt like I wanted death.

"You good?"

"I don't know Lee, he- ." Ali put his hands on my mouth and looked back in my eyes.

"No Nya I'm not asking, I'm telling you that you are." He licked his lips and bent down kissing my neck. I lifted my chin allowing him to continue. Ali stopped and stood straight up and planted a soft kiss on my lips. He pulled away, pressed the down button on the elevator and walked away. Taking my heart with him with just that kiss, Ali had taken a part of me that only Sacario should have.

Chapter 6 Bad to Worse

Lanya

If I thought looking at Sacario lay in a hospital bed was too much, it was killing me to lay beside him and be hiding so much from him. I remember a time when I begged Cario to just be honest with me, however now it was me keeping all the secrets. We hadn't really talked since I told him I was having a baby. I just wanted my husband back.

"Come here ma," Sacario said as if he could read my mind. He pulled me on his chest and ran his hands through my hair. That always gave me chills when he did it.

"Baby I'm sorry, I love you." He says and I feel my heart beating faster. I roll on top of him and kiss his bare stomach.

"Nya I love you and my kids more than I love myself, I should have never flipped on you. But the way I been feeling with this case and my brother, you know they say when someone dies a child is born! I'm just glad Nero A-1 now, but that was stressing me" He rolled me over on my back and placed his hand on my belly and rubbed it. A lump filled my throat. Sacario bent down kissing my stomach and a tear rolled down my face.

"Babe what's wrong? You know I'm gone' love this baby just like I love Deuce and Lyssa. Just like I love you and I do love you," he says kissing my belly again.

"Cario you said you didn't want another baby," I said pulling away.

"So fuckin what, you know I was just frustrated Nya." He roars causing me to flinch. Sacario pulls me back and holds me tighter.

"I'm sorry baby, I really am and if I could take it back on all I love I would...

"Now come give ya man some of that fat pregnancy pussy." I scooted back again, damn near falling on the floor. "Come here, what you doing?" Sacario asked pulling me to his chest.

God how am I gone tell this man after he told me he didn't want the child in anger, I marched to the abortion clinic and killed his baby. Shit it was bad enough that I couldn't tell him about the 12 letters that Keith had sent me from jail. Hell I hadn't told him that Keith use to rape me, fuck my mind was racing. Nikki was calling every day, she knew that Sacario was out of jail, the court case was coming up and now I had kissed Lee. I was about to explode, tears rolled down my cheek and I felt drained.

"Baby what's wrong?" Cario asked and I dug my face in his chest and start to really cry.

"I saw you with her Cario, I saw the way..,"

"Babe who?" He says cutting me off making me feel stupid.

"Dammit Cari you know who; that bitch walks in the room and you fuckin light up, God you didn't even stop me from leaving."

"Oh fuck Nya I'm sorry, the bullets in my fuckin side prevented me from hopping out the bed and chasing you. That's why I sent a bodyguard and my fuckin brother to keep you safe. Fuck Nya, I'm here with you. Shit Nya, I love you. That woman is my lawyer. You have got to let this insecure shit go. It's you that I married, you that I give houses, cars and even children to."

Sacario had me feeling like crap, I was hurting and I just wanted the pain to go away.

"Nya I love you," he says and I lose it.

"Well don't, because while you was loving me so much, you were giving other bitches babies. Killa I hate you. You gave another woman a child and let me think I'm your all. God, sitting here lying to me when you know you fucking the bitch Olivia." Sacario jumped out the bed trying to grab me, but I kept running to the other side. Both the house phone and his cell phone were ringing and he was so busy trying to grab me he didn't care.

"Answer the phone Cario, it's probably yo bitch."

"Baby talk to me, I didn't know Nikki was pregnant until you said something, then she disappeared." That comment stopped me in my tracks. I didn't even know he knew about Nikki.

"You knew about this fuckin child?" I ask dropping to my knees and he bends to stand me up.

"Baby I'm sorry, but I have done my best to keep you out of it."

"That's the problem, I'm yo wife, I should be the first person you put in it. But I guarantee that Ali and Dinero knew?"

"Babe it's not like that."

"Then what is it like Cario? Tell me because in this moment I hate you, I fuckin hate you so much that I killed my baby!" I yelled before I thought about what I was saying, and the look in Sacario's eyes were so sad. I guess he back handed me before I even had a chance to think. I flew into the wall and blood rushed out my nose. The fall must have knocked me out because I opened my eyes to hear my son's voice.

"Move little man," I hear Sacario as my eyes close.

"Mommy don't die," Deuce cries and I can't even keep my eyes open.

Ali

"Nigga what did you do!? I came here to tell you that they sending them boys so you won't be caught off guard and you killing yo wife?"

"Man fuck that bitch." Sacario says On all I love I'm not a jealous man, but when I say it kills me to watch my brother dog his wife, that shit kills me. I walked in looking at this nigga Killa standing in the middle of his bed room Nya on the floor and they're son in tears and I wanna fuck this nigga up. I try talking to him but his light brown skin is red and I can tell he's not in his right mind.

58

"Nigga get some clothes on so I can take you in." I walk him to the closet wanting desperately to check on Nya, but I can't. Sacario walks in the closet and I walk over to Deuce, lifting him in my arms and assure him his mother will be ok. As I rock my nephew I turn to see Sacario marching out the closet, his gun in hand and he is moving like he's on a mission.

"Deuce go get uncle a juice," I tell my nephew standing him to his feet. As soon as my nephew leaves I grab my brother who has a gun in his unconscious wife's face, yelling for her to get up. This nigga had to be high on some shit. I finally grabbed the gun away from him and slide it down in my waist band.

"Nigga chill, what happened?" And like that Killa went from zero to sixty. He flopped down on the bed and started to breathe heavy.

"She killed my seed."

"Nigga what you mean?" I ask feeling dumb.

"This dumb bitch got an abortion." He says and I understand why he so livid.

"Killa that's yo wife. I don't care what she did, she still yo wife." I tell him walking in the closet pulling out clothes for this nigga to put on. I won't lie, I was pissed as fuck these niggas killing babies and I can't even meet a woman to give me a seed. Killa got dressed and walked out the room to check on the kids, so I knew I should check on Nya. I check her pulse and lift her in my arms. She smells like cherry candy, I just want to place my lips on her. Nonetheless I lay her down and cover her body with the blanket.

Sacario walks back in the room, his eyes heavy.

"I never meant to put hands on her Lee. I mean I use to watch daddy beat my momma till she couldn't move and I promised I would never be him. But I won't lie, sometimes Nya take me there and it scares the fuck out of me. I never want to be like Pops, but I don't want to lose my wife, she my life." Killa say and he walks over to Nya lifting her body and sitting down so he could hold her. He bends down kissing her face and I instantly envy my brother.

"Come on nigga, let me take you in."

"Nigga for what trial starts next week?"

"They got a witness, so it's new charges and I told them I would bring you in and we only got forty minutes to get there. I been calling yo ass for like two hours."

"Ouch," I hear and I look at Nya trying to move and Killa pulling her back down. He stands up and lays her on the pillow.

"Babe I'm sorry," Killa says to Nya and she turns her head to not look at him. "Yo Nya, I am going call my momma to come sit with you and the kids." I tell her and she pulls herself up.

"Why what's wrong?"

"I got to turn myself in, but it will be ok." Killa said and Nya starts to cry. She holds her arms out reaching for him and he bends down picking her up like a child.

The fuck, I think to myself. Tom and Jerry muthafucka's, killing each other and now they best friends, fuck outta here. I think looking at him hug her as she cries. As sick as it makes me, I know that I'm jealous as fuck.

"Let's go nigga, she good."

"Cario are we good?" Nya ask and he walks back kissing her lips.

"Yeah I'll fix it Nya, I love you."

I walk out the room and down the stairs looking at my nephew sitting on the stairs like he's sad.

"Is daddy going to go to jail?" I can't even answer him. For an eight year old this nigga smart as fuck.

Sacario

Seeing my wife hit the floor, I knew we were a done deal. The man she was turning me into, is a nigga I couldn't look at in the mirror. Ali walks in my room "Yo Lee grab Deuce and take to O and Kym. I'm gone' call Liv and let her take me in, I need yo hands to stay clean. You good," I ask my wife and she nods yes and I bite down on her bottom lip.

"You hate me?" Nya asked and I shake my head no, not really knowing how I'm feeling. My phone rings pulls me out my thoughts and I look at Olivia's number. Nya holds her hands out for me and I stand and answer the phone.

"Sup Liv?" I say watching Nya's face turn upside down. She rolls her eyes and turns over on her stomach and I can't help but to wonder why she is so insecure when I have never loved any woman, but her.

"Yeah Liv, Lee called you coo!I will meet you at the 9th precinct in the morning." I end my call and lean against the wall looking at Nya, almost all of me just wants to go make love to my wife, but on the other hand, I'm so fuckin pissed that she would kill our child.

"I'ma go check on Alyssa and then sleep in the guest room."

"Yeah alright Cario," Nya says and before I can get out the door I hear her whimpers.

"Nya what you want from me?" It's a long silence as I stand in the door way listening to her breathe as if she is trying to catch her breath.

"Take the rings, the money, the cars and this fuckin house Cario, none of it means a damn thing if I don't have your fuckin heart." She yells causing me to turn and look at her. Her body slumped over and her hands are through her thick hair. I know I love my wife, but I refuse to be some pussy nigga to prove it. I walk over to our bed and lay besides her grabbing her face so she has no choice but to look at me.

"Lanya this is my last time telling you this, you are it for me! Yes I made a mistake with a few hoes, but that's all they were; hoes. You have my last name and my heart, no one can change that but you. Now if you want us to work baby, you need to get over this insecurity or bipolar cry baby bull shit that you going through. I need to know that you my Bonnie when shit go down."

"Cario have I ever gave you a reason to feel that I wasn't yo ride till we die?" I laughed at her poor use of slang and kissed her forehead.

"It's ride or die."

"Nigga that sound dumb, if I can ride with you I damn sure will die for you, why I got to pick an or?" She says crossing her arms over her chest and poking her lips out. I couldn't help but laugh.

"Olivia has nothing on you Mrs. Alton and she never will." I tell her bringing her face to mine kissing her like it was the last kiss we would share, because a part of me felt as if it may be for a while.

I woke up with my wife in my arms feeling like I did when we first met. She was holding on to me so tight I was surprised that I could still breathe. I kissed her forehead, showered, dressed and grabbed my key's before Lanya spoke.

"So you weren't going to wake me?"

"Nah babe you need yo rest, the baby still sleep and Kym got Deuce, so—,"

"So you feed me all that shit about being a down bitch, but then you leave and not allow me to play my role as that chick."

"Really, you want to fight now Nya?"

"No baby I don't," she stood up and walked over to me hugging me with every bit of strength she had, her body was shaking and tears were on her face.

"I don't want to get a call Sacario, I'm your wife."

"I don't want you there!" I tell her, kissing her and pulling away. There was nothing more to be said, I grabbed my phone and walked out the room, leaving my wife standing in that very same spot.

Olivia was looking good as fuck in that all white suit, I won't lie at times she matched my fly but she was still no Nya, and could never be the other half of me. But I would be lying if I said I hadn't smashed a few times. Liv kisses my cheek pulling me from my thoughts.

"Babe before we go in you should know they have a witness. She has no physical evidence but because of who you are, they are going to allow her before a grand jury to see if your case should go to trial."

"What charges, and do we know who she is?"

"Renae something is her name. But she claims to have been engaged to you and involved in a lot of your business, and was there when you planned a few murders."

Olivia had an inquisitive look on her face, like because she was my lawyer I was going to start confessing all my sins.

"You know who she is?" I shook my head no but of course I knew who she was.

Renae was the white chick I had started kicking it with when I got out of jail. Lanya was with that bum ass Dom nigga, and I just needed someone to chill with. Before I knew it, Renae and I were engaged and her true colors started to show. I guess mine did to, because as much as I thought I could move on past my wife, Nya is my soul mate and truth is, there will never be another woman that can do it for me. Renae didn't deal with it well, and I guess I should have put two in that bitch's head when she bleached my clothes and stabbed me. But shit I really didn't think she was crazy enough to come back, and start trouble.

"Sacario, you ready?" Olivia asked breaking my thoughts as we walked into the court house. It went faster than I thought it would, I was processed and cuffed before I even had a chance to realize what was going on.

Chapter 7: Death or Divorce

Lanya

Sacario had me fucked up if he thought that I was gone' sit on the side lines and wait till Olivia called me. That's never been me. He said he want a Bonnie to his Clyde, a Juliet to his Romeo, but last I checked them dudes ended up dead from lack of communication. That's not gone' be us, when we die, it's gone' be because niggas was just gunning for us. I knew it would make no sense to call Olivia, because despite what Cario said that bitch had it out for me, and asking Lee or Nero would be just like asking Cario. My best bet was David. He was working for the DA's office now, and that would work in my favor. He agreed to meet me at the court house at 12pm, that's when Sacario would be arraigned. I dropped Alyssa off over Ali's mother's house, I had only met her once but after Sacario had been arrested she felt now was as good of time as any to come around.

She wasn't Ali's birth mother, truth was no one knew who Ali's mother was, just that he was found in a house where three people had died from an overdose of bad heroin. Not something Lee really ever talked about, but Doris was a good woman and from what I understood she was a big influence in both Lee and Sacario's life. We made very little small talk, before she hugged me and watched me walk to my car.

I met David at the court house, and he looked as good as I remembered. Dressed in a blue pinstriped suit and his full frame was so sexy to me. Truth was I always had a bit of a crush on David, he was how I pictured Sacario would be if he wasn't in the streets.

"Hello beautiful," David says pulling me from my daydream.

"Hey love, how are you?" I asked hugging him, I could tell he was as happy to see me as I was to see him, but I wouldn't show it. I followed David in the court room, watching him in action had me wishing I had finished Law school, however that was my past. Finally Sacario's name was called and he was brought to the front of the room. Olivia wasn't far behind in a pleated white suit and Jimmy Choo heels. I saw her, but was unsure if she could see me, she was leaning up against Sacario whispering in his ear and I wanted to gag. Olivia and the judge spoke back and forth, while a female DA described a man that I didn't know. The words monster, killer and evil were used and it killed me want to defend my husband.

"Well is anyone here on his behalf?" The judge asked and Olivia quickly said no, I stood but David pulled me back down.

"I am sir, I'm his wife." I say and Sacario and Olivia both look at me.

"What is she doing here?" Olivia asks Sacario loudly, and I feel as if maybe I had made the wrong choice.

"Step forward young lady." The judge says and I do. He looked me over and smirked, "Bail set at two million dollars!" He says and bangs his gavel. I looked at Olivia suck her teeth and whisper in Sacario's ear, and I just have to get the fuck out of there. I don't even bother waiting for David as I quickly rush into the hall way.

"He doesn't want bail paid," Olivia says walking over to me and I need to get away from this bitch. I walk outside and down to the lot where I parked my car, I popped the trunk and pulled out a duffle bag that probably weighed as much as I did. I couldn't carry it so I just dragged it inside. Yeah it was risky as hell to bring cash into a jail house, IRS on yo ass if you spend more than five grand without proof of income, but I had that covered. I stopped at the Diamond Broker, before I got to the court house and sold every bit of jewelry I owned and two of my cars that I knew I had no use for.

"What's that you got?" David asked lifting the bag from the ground and sitting it on the metal detector.

"Five point seven million dollars in large bills," I replied walking to the cashier.

It took over forty minutes for the cashier to get over the fact that I was paying in cash, but she handed me forms to fill out, and with the rest of my cash I walked over to the bench and sat down and waited for my husband to be released.

"Hey bay," I said standing to greet Sacario, but he was mean mugging me and Olivia was still by his side. I lifted the bag onto the bench and pulled out six stacks of neatly wrapped cash and handed it to her.

"You're fired, I got it from here." I tell her

"Little girl please," she says refusing the money and I look to Cario.

"Thanks Liv, your no longer needed," he says and I feel a huge weight lifted from my shoulders.

"You can't be serious!?"

"Yeah I am," he says and I couldn't hide the smile that spread across my face. I turned hugging my husband, as we watch Olivia stump up the hall. It baffled me that she didn't protest but I was over joied being in my husbands arms I didn't have time to care; when I felt a tap on my shoulder. I read Sacario's face before I even turned around.

"What are you doing here?" Sacario asks and I slowly turn around looking at a woman holding her stomach and looking me over like I'm the side bitch.

Sacario

This day had gone from bad to worse in a matter of minutes. I stood looking at a blast from my past, and my first reaction was, why was she here? Renae stood in front of me rubbing her belly, and I could just see the tears fall down Lanya's face.

"God I can't anymore Cario, I can't," she cried out handing me the duffle bag and running out of the court house leaving me to face a bitch that had just signed her own death certificate.

"What you want?" I ask her keeping my eye on my wife as she walks out the door.

"I want you to regret leaving me for that whore." She says and I laugh, stepping away from her to catch up with Nya.

She standing outside with the lawyer friend of hers, and his arms are wrapped around her. I'm instantly ready to kick both they're asses.

"Fuck wrong with you?"

"I can't Cario, everything I do is never enough."

"Enough for what, Nya I didn't know that bitch was gone be there?"

"And I guess that's not yo baby she carrying?"

"It's not, I haven't seen that bitch in like ten months." She sucked her teeth, kissed the lawyer niggas face and ran down the stairs of the court house.

"Nya I'm not gone chase ya ass," I yell chasing her down the stairs. I grab her arm and she smacks me, I grab her other arm and pull her into me, "babe I love you!"

"Then why you keep hurting me Killa?" She says snatching away and walking towards the parking lot.

Chapter 8: The Cop, the Killer and the Dope boy

Ali

It had been a minute since I really had to put in work, I think we had been spoiled, having niggas to do shit for us all the time. But I only trusted one nigga outside my brothers, and that was the nigga Saint, but I had sent that nigga to Chicago on some get money shit, so it was up to me and my brothers to clean house.

I pulled up in front of Dinero's old spot, it was the only place we all felt safe to talk. I saw that he and Sacario were already there, and I really didn't feel like going inside. Whenever we held these meetings, we always ended up fighting and me being told to sit on the side lines. Fuck it, might as well get the shit done and over with, I thought to myself, hopping out my truck and making my way inside.

"Sup bitch ass?" Dinero said soon as I walk in the door.

"I got ya bitch ass," I say walking to the drink cart and pouring me a drink.

"So what's up?" Dinero ask, and I drop my head.

"So you know they got this Renae bitch and she spitting all types of information. She got old account numbers, dates and some creditable shit."

I look at Sacario, who is sitting to the side texting.

"Nigga do you hear me?"

"Yeah nigga I heard you, call Saint and get the shit handled."

"He's out of town and we need an outsider, this has to be someone that can't be traced to us."

"So let me do it!" A woman's voice says walking in the door. We all sat up looking at Nya. She was dressed in all black, like she was ready for war.

"What the fuck you doing here?" Sacario asked walking over to Lanya, she walked away and sat in between Dinero's legs.

"O tell him to let me do it, he says he wants a down bitch then let me prove I am."

"Nya you sound stupid," Sacario said and I laugh.

"Ali hear me out. I have no record, I am a law student and I know how to lie with a straight face if it came to that, but most of all who do the three of you trust more than you trust me? I would die before I let anything happen to either of you."

"Hell no," Sacario roared. Dinero shook his head no and as much as I wanted to say no I knew Nya was right.

"I say yeah," standing to my feet looking at my bothers give me a mean mug.

"Nigga you have lost yo fuckin mind, you think my wife...."

"Nigga I think she our best bet unless I'm gone do it!?"

"You crazy as fuck, I'm not letting her do shit!"

"How you gone stop me?" Nya yelled out standing to her feet walking over to Sacario, "I'm doing it and if that means we are over because of it, so be it, I rather have a nigga I can love from afar then a nigga I can't even see." Dinero stood up and grabbed Nya sitting her back down on his lap and I couldn't help but laugh. Nya was the only one who could pull Sacario hoe card and leave him speechless.

"Do that shit and we over."

"Good Killa, I was sick of yo ass anyway!" Nya said and just like that she was crying. I couldn't hold my laughter. As hard as she played, that nigga could bring her to tears and she could turn him into a pussy.

"Man come here," Sacario yelled and Lanya ran to his arms and I hit Dinero as we both fell to the floor laughing. The fuck, I couldn't with my brother and his wife.

"Man is she in or out?" Dinero asked still laughing and I waited for the answer.

Chapter 9: Sacario

Lanya

So did you know in Spanish Sacario means hit man, I guess his mother even knew that her son would be a killer? I had never saw anyone get killed or even killed anyone myself, but here I stood at a Holiday Inn Express in Dearborn, Michigan with a red wig on, a black baseball cap and navy blue sweats. I took my hotel room key from the clerk trying not to show how nervous I was. Although I felt as if the air had been sucked out of my body and in any given second I could fall apart.

Truly I didn't know why I was so nervous; Ali had come up with a master plan. He made me leave my phone at home, where he or Sacario would call Kym, and the GPS would appear that I was at home. All I had to do was check in the Holiday Inn, wait till midnight and go across the street to the Day's Inn and kill the Renae chick.

I really wasn't fond of the bitch, thinking of our last meeting I really had no remorse for her. Our last encounter had been one of the worst days of my life. The day I became aware of my mother's death, also the day I damn near lost my own life, as well as my daughters. On the bright side, it was the day my husband came home. It still didn't change the fact that this Anna Nichole look alike was so bitter that she felt that she had to snitch. The worse part of all was the fact that the woman was pregnant and with the luck I had been having, the child most likely belong to Sacario.

I won't lie, it's not a night I don't cry wondering why I stay with a man clearly out to hurt me. I walk into my room of the Holiday Inn Express, taking in the cheap room.

"Not what you use to?" I hear and I damn near jump out of my skin turning to look at my husband.

"You're not supposed to be here Cario!" I tell him wrapping my arms around his waist, so happy that he is there.

"Nya that's not my baby," he says as if he's in my head.

"I didn't say it was!"

"I need you to know that if you plan on going through with this. Baby if you don't want to I will understand, and trust I will find another way out." I didn't respond, I just hugged my husband feeling his warm body against mine.

"You know you my world?" He asked and I release his waist and stand up on my tippy toes to kiss his lips. I pull away looking in his eyes before I walk over to the window and stare out. All that Sacario and I had been going through I knew that my love was true, but I was so unsure that I was anything more to him than just a bitch he wanted to keep quiet.

"What you thinking Nya?" Sacario asked and how can I bare to tell my husband, my only thought is if I am strong enough to walk away from him?

Sacario pulled me onto the bed and held me tightly. I always felt so safe there.

At midnight I didn't want to get up and I felt as if he didn't want to let me go. However he did let me go and I moved quickly slipping on my heavy timberland boots and covering my head with the baseball cap. Once outside I covered my head with the hood from my jacket, kept my head low as Sacario had instructed and tried to breathe as my life felt like it was moving in slow motion. I pulled the burner phone from my pocket that already had a text from another burner phone reading the room number. I closed my eyes as I approached the room wondering what could go wrong.

I knocked on the door and that's when I really got worried. When there was no answer I knocked harder.

"What?" Renae asked yanking the door open. We were now face to face and I knew what I had come to do, but I wanted answers, like why. Her mouth parted when she looked at me then I guess she saw the gun that rested in my hand and she started to scream and run towards the back of the room. That's when I realized the baby bump she had at the court house was no longer there. I lifted the gun.

"Put the phone down," I tell her and she continues to try and dial the number. I run up on her and place the gun to her head snatching the phone. My hands shake and I really want to kill her, but I can't. Renae grabs for the gun and tosses me to the floor. We tussle for just a second before I look up at the gun that I was to use on her is now pointed at me.

"What are you waiting on?" I ask. I hear two pops and I cover my face trying not to scream, feeling warm droplets on my face. I fear opening my eyes, but at this point I know I have to.

"Man they sent you to do this, what the hell were they thinking?" Saint asked, pulling me from the floor.

"Clearly they didn't trust me to do it," I say in anger.

"NO I didn't trust you to do it," Saint says taking his shirt and wiping my face.

"Strip," Saint tells me and I can't.

"LANYA I SAID STRIP!" He yells at me and I do as he has told me. I rush taking off my clothes and slipping into a jogging suit that Saint has provided. He takes the clothes from me, gaze into my eyes and I won't lie I was a bit lost in his. He kissed my forehead and sent me on my way so that he can finish what I came to do.

Ali

Am I my brother's keeper, if not me then who? I had been cleaning up Killa's and Nero's mess since we were kids. Why should today be any different? I knew they wouldn't allow Nya to go through with it, but if I made it seem like it was the last resort they would trust me. Nonetheless I knew Nya's kindness would never allow her to take another's life. That was one of the things I loved about Nya, she was no killer. I believed that she wanted to prove to us she was a part of our family, but she was nothing like us, or her brother. Saint was a stone cold killer that I had parts in trainin training myself. I often wondered how such a delicate flower could exist around such hard stones, but Nya had proven herself time after time again. I grabbed her as she walked towards the Holiday Inn looking as if she were in a trance. "It's our secret," I tell her hugging her tightly.

"Cario doesn't know?" She asks in a state of shock.

"No and he never will, not if you don't want him to." I tell her placing her in the truck and pulling off as quickly as I could. We all agreed that we wouldn't see each other tonight and that Nya would spend the night with me, just in case they brought Sacario in for questioning.

We pulled up to my house and Lanya was quiet. I just parked and got out, walking to her side to help her down.

"I'm good Lee, I got this." She tells me and it pisses me off how stubborn she could be.

"Whatever Nya," I say walking to the door and letting us in.

"Make yourself at home, I'm gone run you some bath water."

"I can take a shower in the guest room," she says and I laugh.

"Alright Nya, no problem, this not yo first time here. I'm going to go shower and lay down." I tell her, kissing her forehead and running up the stairs.

"NYA!" I yell from the top of the stairs.

"Yes!?"

"The burner phone, where is it?"

"Saint took it," I nod my head and go back into my bedroom, I'm not trying to shake the thoughts that invade my mind.

After a hot shower I walk into my bedroom with the smell of food lingering in the air. As I walk towards my closet and Lanya is smiling at me.

"Y'all all have the same tattoo or just you and Cario?" She ask me pointing to the prayer hands on my shoulder, with the words brother's keeper beneath it.

"We all have them," I tell her dropping my towel and slipping on ball shorts.

"I made you a plate." Nya says still looking my body up and down. I neatly put my things away and lay across the bed looking at Nya sit on the floor and eat whatever is in her bowl.

"What you eating?" I ask her.

"I made some stir fry, um so your kitchen is spotless and so is your room, are you anal." Nya ask and I smile grabbing her bowl from her hand and tasting the food. I hated eating behind people, but something made me want to share with her.

"What's this again, shit kind of good?" "I'm glad, give me my damn food Lee." She says standing from the floor, climbing on the bed and grabbing the bowl. I wouldn't let it go. Ripping it from her hands I took the fork and held the food out for her to take a bite. She looked at the fork for a second and rolled her eyes. "I'm a baby now," she says eating the bite of food. I sat the bowl on my bedside table and pulled Nya on top of me.

"Yeah you are." We were looking into each other's eyes and I could tell she didn't want to move either. Reaching my lips to hers I kissed her. Did I know what I was doing was wrong, yes however it felt so good. It felt as if Nya was a part of me, and she wasn't fighting what we had.

"Lee what are we doing?" Lanya ask as she lightly kiss my chest, I run my hands through her hair.

"Whatever you wanna do Nya," I tell her thinking about the tattoo on my back.

Lanya moved her lips from my chest back up to my lips. Her soft skin felt so good against my rough hands.

"Fuck Lee, he's your brother!" She says rolling to the other side of the bed and balling into a ball.

"You don't think I know that!" I pulled her to face me, her slanted dark brown eyes and golden brown skin turned me on. Damn I was in love with my brother's wife. I had a million things I wanted to say but I didn't, I released her face and we just stared at each other.

"Hell y'all looking at?" Killa says as he walks into my room. My heart feels as if it had stopped.

"Baby what you doing here?" Lanya jumped out the bed and onto Killa so fast, it was like we hadn't just come close to making love.

"Thought we agreed yo ass would stay home till tomorrow."

"Nigga we did but I missed my wife." He tells me kissing Lanya's neck.

"Baby get yo stuff so we can go home. I need you tonight." Killa tells Nya slapping her ass watching her walk out my bedroom.

"She tastes good right?" My brother says to me, letting me know he knows that we kissed.

"Nigga fuck that mean?" I asked Killa who had his eyebrow raised.

"You my brother, just don't forget that." He tells me walking out the room leaving me in a daze.

Chapter 10: Fly on the Wall

Lanya

"CARIO!" I screamed as I woke up once again alone in my bed. My back was covered in sweat and my heart was racing. Renae is all I would see when I closed my eyes. In addition, my body was shaking and I missed my husband. Yes I thought about how close I had come to being with his brother, but it was a reason I had stopped myself. I belonged to Sacario completely, and I didn't want another man to feel my body.

I looked up at the clock that now said 3 am and felt the empty spot besides me. A loud sigh escaped my body as I dialed my husband's phone.

"Sup ma?" He says damn near out of breath and my heart flip flops.

"Hey babe, you coming home?"

"Yeah I'll be there; I just got mad work on the floor." He says blowing me off like I'm some random woman. It wasn't hard to see since the night at Lee's house Sacario had been distant. I guess I was to blame.

After all it was me that had broken all the rules, and although he didn't say it, I knew that Sacario knew what I had done. It was no going to sleep now. I turned on the television and began to watch; but truth was it was really watching me because I was in deep thought.

"What you thinking about baby?" Sacario says walking into our bedroom. His hands full of bags as he bends to kiss my face.

"Thinking about you," I tell him eyeballing his packages.

"What's in your hand?" He smiles and opens the first bag handing me a container of food. He then hands me a real spoon. I stared at the spoon and smiled.

"You know me so well," I say reaching up to kiss him. He sits on the bed beside me and pulls out another container and a fork. He begins to eat as do I, however every time I look up Sacario's eyes are on me like he has a question for me.

"What is it Cari?"

"Do you still love me Nya?" He asked with a serious look on his face.

"You know I do." I tell him moving my food to the side of the bed and crawling over towards him kissing his face. He grabs my hands and pulls me onto his lap, he smells like Sean John I am King, weed and Double mint gum. His scent alone gave me chills.

"Nya, why have you never asked me to leave the game?" I pulled myself up and looked in his eyes. My first thought was, could I even ask him that.

"Seriously Cario?"

"Yeah babe, I know these last few years have not been easy for you, most women would ask a nigga to leave the game but not you, is it the money?" He asked and now my guards were really up, I rarely asked Cario for money and I had always worked for what I wanted or needed, his money was just a perk.

"No Killa it's not the fuckin money, it's not the life, you were in this game when I met you. When I chose to be with you I knew the game was what u did, so why would I want to change you. I know when you ready to fuckin walk away, you will." I tell him climbing over him grabbing my food and tossing it in the trash. He had pissed me off and I just wanted to sleep. I grabbed a pillow from the bed and the throw blanket from my chase by the window. I rarely sat on my chase, but after our fight

I didn't want to lay next to a man who thought I was after his money.

"You sleeping over there?" Cario asked as I covered my body and closed my eyes tightly. I didn't try to stop the tears as they began to fall, I loved my husband and he doubted that. No matter what I did I would never be good enough.

"Alright I'm out then." He says and I try not to care. I can hear him move around. He picks up his keys and dials a number on his phone.

"Yo bro I need a place to lay low, my fuckin wife tripping." I hear him say and I turn to face him.

"I'm trippin' Cario, you the one walking out on me yet again. You probably came home to fight just so you can go to her!"

I jumped off the chase and cut my eyes at him. I rushed to the closet, anger consumed me. The questions, the pulling away all made sense, he was leaving me. I thought to myself walking into our closet. It was the size of a master bedroom. I looked at Sacario's clothes neatly hanging and began to rip everything down.

"Take it all, everything. You leaving Cari take it all! Take it and go to her, that's what you been dying to fuckin do. Get everything and go to yo fuckin bitch Sacario." I yelled dropping to the floor. I couldn't take a moment more of hurt.

"Fuck are you talking about Nya?"

"Go to yo bitch Cario let her fuck you, clearly she gives you what I don't!"

"She always has Nya." He says and I want to die. Sitting up looking at my husband, we stare into each other's eyes. Sacario walks over to me and rips me from the floor. I fight to sit up, but he is almost 300 pounds of solid muscle, so the fight is short lived.

"You are my fuckin wife Nya." He lifts my night shirt ripping my already thin panties off me. I continued to fight, but he didn't care his hand slipped around my throat and Sacario forced me to look at him.

"You are my wife, my bitch, my hoe and anything I want you to be." He pulled down his jogging pants with his free hand and plunged inside of me. He went deep and hard and it felt so good, but I still was so mad I didn't want him touching me. He placed my legs on his shoulders and went deeper and harder. I pulled away, but Sacario pulled me back.

"Do you understand me Nya?" Sacario yelled, as he went in me deeper.

"You mine, you belong to me, this pussy belongs to me, you understand!?" He said holding my face still so I was forced to look in his eyes as he fucked me.

"You hear me?" I refused to answer, I just nodded my head.

"You hear me Nya?"

"Yeah! Yeah I hear you Killa." I said out of breath and shaking. Sacario smiled as he erupted inside me.

"Don't forget that shit." He said climbing off me disappearing into the bathroom. I just laid in the bed as he left me.

Sacario

My wife had a way of acting like a fuckin brat. But she was my brat. Nonetheless since I saw her kissing my brother, I had been wondering if she was tired of me. I knew I had fucked up. Olivia, Renae and of course Nikki. I won't deny I was wondering if maybe she would be happier with my brother.

Lee was my right hand, and I knew he could treat her way better than I could, but I was selfish. I didn't want to see any other man with my wife, and the truth was I loved Nya enough to kill any man who tried to take her from me. Any man. I walked out the bathroom to see Nya laying in our bed, it didn't look like she had moved from the spot I had left her in. I dried off and got dressed. Looking at the clock, I knew I should just get in the bed and lay next to her, but I was still pissed just thinking of another man on her . I grabbed my keys and my phone and walked out the bedroom.

"Walk away Killa, all you know how to do." Nya said and I turn and look at her.

"Yep, long as yo ass know you better not go any damn where," I tell her pulling my phone out and calling Ali. Although I was pissed at him, I needed some place to crash, to think, and Dinero had enough going on with his girl.

Soon as I stepped out of my house, it was like they had been waiting for me. Red and blue lights lit up the entire block and sirens sounded indicating more to come.

"Brah what's going on?" Lee says into the phone.

94

"Sacario Alton, interlock your hands on your head and drop to the ground," a man says through a loud speaker and I look back at the sea of police cars to bring me down. I did as I was told dropping to the ground and cuffing my hands on the back of my head.

Chapter 11... The come up!

7 years later

(Lanya)

I lay on my bed thinking about my life and the shit that I have been through. I went from being this insecure chubby girl in a bad relationship, with a closet full of skeletons that not even I wanted to know about. You couldn't tell me 15 years ago, that I would be the mother of two and living in a huge house with 3 cars in the drive way, and divorced. Never would I think in a million years that all that I fought for would come to an end. I lay on my huge bed and wonder how the hell I got to this place and sad to say I already knew. Tears flow down my face as I think about the look on Sacario's face seven years ago. Nothing hurt worse than the moment that judge said twenty years. I felt myself die. I stood alone in that court room wondering where the fuck his brothers. Where was all that loyalty that they had always preached about? Shit my husband was King, where the fuck was his kingdom!? I tried to give them all the benefit of the doubt; however no one had reached out to me, and when I went to visit Sacario, I was told I was not on his list. I didn't want to break down.

It wasn't until nine months into his stay when I got a phone call. I could hear it in his voice he was hurt! I tried to keep my spirits up as I spoke to him.

"Hey daddy," I purred in the phone.

"Yeah babe you and the kids good; O transfer that cash for y'all?" He asked sounding annoyed to talk to me.

"Yeah babe, but me and the kids good, I'm still not on the list to come see you."

"Fuck Nya, you think I'm worried about a list. Man I'm fuckin locked up!" Sacario yelled and instantly tears fell down my face.

"Sorry Cari I just—,"

"Alright Nya I got to go, Olivia gone be in touch!" My heart dropped.

"OLIVIA!" I yelled but he had ended the call, two days later Ms. Olivia showed up at my house in her brand new Benz and designer suit. She looked like a million bucks and I hated her. There were no pleasantries, just business. She stood in front of me as I looked her flawless body over. She handed me three files. The first were his accounts and business transferal of names. Meaning he wanted everything he owned back in his name, no longer in mine. Second was the deed to the house solely in my name, but third took the cake. Divorce papers already signed. I held my head up to fight the tears that were ready to fall.

"Everything ok?" She says with a small grin and I snap!

"No you show up looking like Barbie in her pink sports car and you telling me my husband wants out of our marriage and you want me to be ok!"

"Look LaKeisha—,"

"First off my name is Lanya, second hand me a pen! We really don't need to have that girlfriend's moment!" I wanted to kill this bitch and Sacario right along with her. She hands me a pen and I want to spaz out. I read over the papers and sign the return of business and hand her the other files.

"Tell my husband he can keep the fuckin house! And if he wants a divorce, don't send his hoe to do his job! Tell me to my fuckin face." I held my hand out guiding her to the door. She looked at me like she was insulted and proceeded out the door. That was my wakeup call. It was in that second that I knew that I had to stand on my own two feet.

It was a long ass ride but seven years later I'm here. I am finally feeling like I'm in a good space. I stand from my bed and walk into my closet. I slip on something simple but cute because I wanted to be ready for when my visitor shows up. As soon as I slip into my six inch Jimmy Choo's, I hear the doorbell. I rush out the room hoping that my son over-protective ass doesn't wake up. I love my baby boy, but at times when I look at him all I see is his father and it hurts a million times more. I run downstairs and opened the door looking at a man that made my skin crawl.

"Hey baby girl," my Uncle Smooth says and I gag. He pulls me in for a hug and I can't even embrace him. I pull away and invite him in.

"Baby girl you stay looking like your mother," he says taking a seat and I roll my eyes.

"Thanks Sean."

"Call me Smooth or uncle, you had no problem saying uncle when you wanted me to take you in." He hissed moving his hands towards my face. He pushes a stray hair behind my ear, and then sits back. I roll my eyes as he reminds me of how I had gotten after Sacario went to jail. I take a deep breath and try to see what he is here for, my heart is racing because he's in my house. He had never been here before. Truthfully I would've like to keep him away from my family, however he was becoming persistent and I truly didn't have anywhere else to turn.

"So baby girl where are those kids I had heard so much about?" He touched my face again and I pulled back. I hated how touchy he was with me.

"They're still asleep it is after all, nine in the morning. I'm truly wondering why you wanted to meet so early?" He sucked his teeth and stood to his feet walking around my house. He began to look at a few of my pictures. He went into his pocket pulled a tooth pick out and slipped it in his mouth. I sighed as he picked up a picture that once hunted me. The picture of my father, his brothers and of course Sacario's father. For years I had always wanted to know the whole story, but Sacario assured me that it was something I should never know.

"You know niece, it still shocks me that you got in the bed with the enemy." He sucked his teeth and paced my house. "My first reaction was to kill you for betraying us, for being with a man that was the cause of the demise of our empire, and the killer of your own father. However, your mother--," He paused again and walked over to me standing me to my feet. He ran his hands down my face. Where he should have stopped, he didn't. He continued to trace my frame, my body shivered as his eyes filled with lust. He licked his lips and I stepped back. He grabbed my arm and pulled me into his space. I could now smell a light smell of liquor on his breath.

"Your mother did a lot for you, when I found out, I was going to kill you. Yo momma got that good pussy." He spoke in a rant, but it was clear what he was telling me.

"Smooth, why are you here?" I snap walking to the bar and pouring me a drink. He laughed like a mad man and stepped in my face. He raised his hand and back handed me. I grabbed my face and he pulled me into his space again.

"All this you have is because of me, the money, the cars and the house. You came to me not being able to pay your rent—." I pulled back and looked him over.

"I didn't have rent, it was a mortgage and I came to you because you were my father's brother and nothing more."

"Watch yo-self little girl, for the last year I have been your bread and butter." I sucked my teeth noticing the taste of blood in my mouth.

"Smooth say what you came to say." He stepped closer to me and I took two steps away.

"Listen little girl, you have shown us that you know a few things about the drug game but I still don't feel as if I can trust you." He snatched my drink from my hand and took a sip. "What I need from you is simple loyalty! I want you to help me take down Dinero with him dead yo—," he paused and smiled. "Killa has no strength on the street and our family will rise again." I was hurt by my husband's choices, but he was still a man I promised my heart, trust and loyalty too. His family was my family, even if I felt on the outs, I couldn't betray them! Could I? I glanced at the stairs watching my son walk out the door. He cut his eyes at me and all I could see was his father's disapproval.

"Done, I will bring you Dinero but trust I know these men; he is the one that will not go down without a fight. And to bring death on any of them is to bring death to your front door." Smooth looked me over and smiled. I walked to the door holding it open so that he can leave. A chill shot down my spine as he walked past me and I knew in that moment that I had to be loyal to my family.

Ali

Life is too short to dwell on the past, so why am I sitting here yet another night nursing a glass of 1800 and sprite. I have no reason to feel guilt. Were it not for me, my family would not have one of the strongest drug empires period. I have covered so much shit, lied to so many people and put my life on hold so that we can be at the top of our game. So why is it that I feel like I could have prevented my brother from doing jail time? I take another sip as the sound of my door bell ringing gets me out my feelings. I down the last of my drink, slam the glass to the table and walk to the door. Before I open it I secure my hand behind my back on my gun and unlock the door. My eyes widen as I look into Lanya's eyes. It had been a while since we had been in the same space, in fact she was the last person I expected to see.

"Can I come in?" She asked in the sexiest tone. I removed my hand from my back and took two steps backwards and allowed her to enter. She was rocking a pair of jeans and a blouse, but the way she looked in it blew my mind. She walked into the living room made herself a drink and sat down.

"What up sis?" I reminded myself that she was my brother's wife. She shot me a fucked up face and rolled her eyes. "Sis aye..."

"Man what's up Nya because you the last person I expected to see here?"

"This is the last place I wanted to be, trust me! I need yo help," the look in her face started to worry me. I poured myself a drink and took a seat and she sat beside me. She looked in my eyes then downed her drink. She scooted closer to me wrapped her arms around my neck and just stared.

"You want me don't you?" She went in for a kiss and I stopped her, as much as I wanted to kiss her and so much more she was my brother's wife. I stood up and downed my drink walking to the other side of the room and taking a seat.

"What's up Nya, what you need?" I asked looking in her perfect brown eyes that were now full of sorrow. I wanted to take her in my arms and make things better but that wasn't my place. I sighed as she started to cry and I stood waving her over. She ran to my arms and truly began to sob. I couldn't help my feelings, lifting her into my arms and carrying her upstairs to my bedroom.

Lanya

I had nowhere else to turn, and truth was I knew Ali had a soft spot for me for years. If anyone would help me it would be him. I knew if I went to Dinero he would act before he thought and go in guns blazing. I needed someone to remain calm, and execute the plan without reporting to Sacario. I knew that neither of them would hide it from Carri, but one out of the two would have to do. I went there to manipulate him, however standing face to face with my husband's other half I almost died. Ali was just a darker shade of Sacario. Ali was standing tall as the green giant, with golden brown skin, huge arms, thick full lips and those eyes that looked like they were kissed with honey. How could I not want to touch or kiss him? After all it had been seven years since a man had touched my body, my kitten purred to be stroked. I shook the thought until he lifted me up in his arms like he was superman. I couldn't help but to think of the first time Sacario carried me in his house, into his bedroom and made insane love to me. I yearned for that feeling again, I just wanted for him to make me feel like a woman. Ali tossed me onto his bed and crawled in between my legs, his lips met mine and he bit down. My nipples got hard and my pussy was soaked. "Umm," I moaned.

"FUCK NYA," he shouted releasing my body and standing to his feet.

"WHAT YOU DOING HERE?" He shouted at me as he looked down at his phone that had just started vibrating.

"A call from federal jail," I hear as he places the phone to his ear and turns the volume down. He presses a button and walks away from me. I paced his bedroom, biting my nails waiting for him to return. He took no time at all walking back into the room holding the phone out for me. I look at him wondering if he had told his brother what I had just done. A tear rolled down my face and I grabbed the phone.

"Hello," I said very softly.

"Yo, fuck wrong?" Sacario yells into my ear and I start to cry even more. The sound of his voice sends fear down my spine and causes my heart to pump a few beats faster.

I clear my throat still looking at Ali, "Nothing!" I say softly.

"Man Nya, why the fuck you ain't been taking my fuckin calls? You sending me money I don't fuckin need and then you at my brother house, what the hell?" I rolled my eyes at Ali listening to Sacario yell at me for being his wife, even though it was his choice to leave me.

"Cario I said for better or worse and I will always give you half of whatever I have, however I don't want to hear yo voice knowing that I'm not even allowed to make the trip to New York to see you. Fuck I don't even know why the fuck you in New York." I sucked my teeth feeling fire in the pit of my stomach.

"Look Nya, I got money I don't need yours, I put that money aside for you and my kids." I looked at the phone, then at Ali as Sacario cut into me.

"First off the money you put aside I have not fuckin touched, I...."

"Watch yo fuckin tone, Nya you are my fuckin—," he paused and rightfully so. If he had said I was his wife I may have lost it. Tears poured down my face. I removed the phone from my face and let the tears just fall.

"NYA," he yells and I wipe my face with the back of my hand and listen to his voice.

"Where you getting all the money from?" I suck my teeth truly not wanting to answer, but I had never lied to my husband.

"Smooth and Dice." Ali's mouth hits the floor and Sacario starts to laugh.

"Are you stuck on fuckin stupid? Fuck is wrong with yo dumb ass, you think they yo family, you think that they not gone-- What the fuck you doing for them Nya? Do you not know that-- ," Sacario was pissed. He just huffed in the phone and I knew his every move as I listened to him breathe.

"Give my brother the fuckin phone!" He ordered, and my body shook.

"Cari I—,"

"Nya give my brother the phone," he says cutting me off.

"I love you Sacario," I cry handing Ali the phone and walking towards the door.

Sacario

The sound of Lanya's voice got my heart pounding and my dick hard. I loved the fuck out of my wife and I missed her with everything I had. Nevertheless I couldn't do ten years knowing that she would be carrying my name. While on the streets, Alton was the only name you wanted, but on paper, in business my name was mud. I didn't want her or my children to carry that burden. I thought she would take it hard but move on. However when I found out that she had start using her bitch ass daddy last name, 'Marks' I had never felt so betrayed in my life. Now to find out not only is she using their last name, but working with them my mind is racing. What else had she done in seven years, was she still the same woman I fell in love with?

"Yo?" My brother's voice pulls me out of my thoughts, however at this point I really don't know what to say.

"What up Cario?" Lee speaks again and I suck my teeth.

"Get me out of here, I don't know what you got to do, I really don't give a fuck just get me out!" I demanded slamming the phone down. I walked away from the calling area and back to the round table, I sat down and knocked on the table and one of the three men dealt me into a game of spades. Now on television you watch and think that people play for food and cigarettes, not here. I was surrounded by some of the biggest Bosses in America. We spoke few words behind the walls but as we sat out in the open for that hour of recreation time, they schooled me on things I never thought that I needed to know. We always sat at the same table, the only round table in the court yard. It was said that a former boss had it put in just for meetings like this. You ever wondered why it is called a round table. the cat Gevonni asked me. at table of kings there can be no head of the table. a table must be round so all are equal. He said I admired that. It would be something I would take back home with me, because although I had been away for seven years I was still King, and inside I still ran the streets. With the help of Olivia I was able to not only know what was going on, on the outside, but supply on the inside. So doing time for me wasn't hard and long as I kept Lanya and the kids out my mind, I was fine. Time went by fast and I was able to do what I needed, but hearing her voice, knowing she switched sides; I felt heavy.

Ali

I could hear the pain in my brother's voice, that shit was unnerving. I knew I had to do what I had to, to get him out of that fuckin hell hole. Despite the fact that on the inside Killa was bringing in five hundred large a month. That wasn't a lot for our team, but we had broken into a world that truthfully I didn't know existed. The sound of the door slamming pulls me from my thoughts. Fuck Nya I think, making a dash down the stairs, I must have jumped down like six of them, I run out the door and outside standing behind her truck as she tries to back out the drive way. Lanya slams on the brakes and rolls down her window. "Move Lee," I hit the back of her truck.

"Get the fuck out the car Nya," she releases the break and the car starts to roll back. I feel my body being moved and I'm ready to fuck her up. I pull out my gun and aim at the window.

"Nya get out the fuckin car." She stops the car and sits there, after maybe two minutes she steps out the truck and slams the door crossing her arms over her chest. I slip my gun back down my jeans and walk over to her. I grab her arm and pull her in the house. The sound of the door slamming knocked the hard look she had off her face. she truly didn't know who the fuck I was and I was bout to show her.

"Nya why are you here, and more importantly why you fuckin with my brother head?" I placed both of my arms on the door locking her in as she forcibly tried to look away.

"Nya what the fuck man?" Tears ran down her face and she reached her hands around my neck.

"No going back Nya!" She hugged me tighter and I knew that the line I had avoided crossing was about to be crossed.

Chapter 12 ... Judge me not

Lanya

My husband is the only man I have ever truly loved, wanted and desired. So looking at his brother with a smile and eyes like his, I wanted him to want me. For my own selfish reasons of course, however all that got me was guilt and another night of loneliness. In addition I rushed out of Lee's place so fast that day I didn't tell him Smooth's plan, so I was still facing the fact that I had to do it on my own. My mind was flooded and the only way I knew to get over such a stressful day was shopping. First I had to head to Flint and assure my uncles that I was still in it with them.

I won't lie I knew who I must be loyal too, but I knew in my gut that trying to pretend that I was loyal to the other side was breaking my heart. Either way it went, in someone's eyes I would be a trader. Hell truth was in my husband's eyes I already was. At this point I'm not sure that I disagree.

I had given the Marks my husband's whole game and because of this, they had truly become powerful enough to take over Detroit. Don't get me wrong, Detroit was nothing to Sacario, Ali or Dinero. They ran Atlanta, Ohio, Mississippi and a few other places. It was just that Detroit was home and if they lost home then everyone would think they were weak.

My drive to Flint was a quick one, it was when I got to Club Ecstasy that my heart began to race. It was so eerie that the club resembled The Boss's Lounge to a T. They even had this chick name Naomi that reminded me of Rachael, she was bossy and clung to my uncle Dice like he was the last slice of cake at a birthday party.

"Hey Naomi, Smooth here?" I ask walking into the bar, my heart was racing but I tried to relax but all I could think is what I would say to my uncle. A hand wrapped around my waist and I felt lips on my neck. I pulled away but was forced back. I turned to see who was invading my space, when my uncle stood before me with a smile on his face.

"Hey baby girl, how was your day?" He asked and another man's arm was still wrapped around me like it belonged there.

"It was fine thanks for asking," I replied finally pulling away and looking face to face with one of the most handsome men I had laid eyes on that was not related to my husband.

He was just a little over six feet because he and my uncle were about the same height. His skin was a perfect brown, the color of melted caramel, he had a slim look to him, however he had on a Jordan T shirt that said different. His arms poked out and I understood why biceps were called guns. He had knocked me dead with those boys. I shook it off and tried to have a displeasing look on my face, but the way he was biting on his lips had my nipples hard and my pussy wet as ever.

"What's up baby girl?" The man mocked my uncle and I sucked my teeth.

"Not ya baby and I'm far from ya girl." I said with venom in my voice. He stepped in closer and I got a look at his single dimple and his perfect white teeth.

"Nah you right mami, you are no baby and very clear that you all woman. So with that said you need to be mine." Ugh he was so cocky, and it was turning me on.

"Boy bye, you couldn't afford me," I said walking over to my uncle. The man grabbed my hand and laughed.

"Baby girl clearly yo uncle has not told you who the fuck I am—," I put my hand over his lips and smiled. "No but he has told you who I was because you know he's my uncle, so you need to fall the hell back. Because in case you didn't know, I'm the princess and this right here I'm next in line for." I say waving my hand so he could look at the bar. He grabbed my hand and pulled me in and then bent to my ear he placed his lips on my neck and kissed it, then like a vampire he bit down. I tried not to scream out but it hurt like the devil. He removed his teeth from my flesh and I still felt them.

"See what you need to know is; they don't call me Money cause I'm a broke nigga! And as for you being the princess, I'm the King of Flint. Yo uncle didn't have to tell me shit. Cuz yo daddy left this shit to me. Now wit that being said, you know you belong by my side running this shit." I sucked my teeth and took two steps back.

"You know my father, well knew him?" I questioned the man who was now caressing my hand. "Yeah I knew ya pops, he practicality raised me since I was 12. He sent me to Flint to start this shit when he got killed." He looked to my Uncle Smooth and with a simple nod my uncle approved.

"Your name again, I missed it?"

"I didn't toss that shit, the streets call me Money but you can call me Jayce that's what my momma named me." He said and I shot him a smile. I didn't know what I thought about Jayce, but him being in the game changed all my plans.

"Uncle we need to talk." I said turning away from Jayce to Smooth.

"Shoot baby girl, I'm all ears." Smooth says and I look back at Jayce.

"Alone Uncle," he smiled and before he could reply Jayce was pulling me back to him.

"Didn't you hear me say this was my shit? So whatever you have to say—," my uncle raised his hand cutting Jayce off and I was relieved.

"Baby girl you do that favor I asked for?"

"That's why I'm here uncle, I need time, and I will talk to him at my daughter's birthday party. I don't speak to O but however I know he will be there for my kids." Smooth stepped in my face and I began to feel trapped. I took a deep breath and closed my eyes as my Uncle Smooth ran his hands through my hair. I pulled away and walked out the oreo cookie stance the men had placed me in. My uncle smiled, nodded his head and vanished like he was Casper. I waisted no time following suit, as I exited the bar Jayce grabbed my hand and pulled me back, I felt weak and I knew I had to take control. I pushed back and he held on tighter.

"Look mama fight all you want but I get what I want, and you are what I got my eyes on." He released me and walked away. I reached in my purse, pulled out my keys and ran towards my car. This day had to get better.

Money

Bitch clearly had no idea who I was so (Allow me to introduce myself...) I can't believe that Silk's daughter grew up to be that bad. I remember when that nigga Silk had me dropping cash to his wife. I couldn't be no older than 16, so she had to be 12 and trust she was not looking like that. I guess milk really does a body good. AMEN. I thought to myself the whole time she stood before me in those white jeans and red heels. Damn had a nigga ready to fuck. Man I don't chase women, shit in fact it had been a minute since I had been in a relationship. Not since my sons mother Nikki died, no other woman has really caught my attention; that is until tonight. I step in my crib to see my son lounged on the couch, him and his little home boy playing video games.

"Yo nigga, you been here all day?" I ask Jayson with my eyebrow raised.

"Nah pops," he says tossing chips in his mouth. I look his home boy over and he looks so familiar.

"Yo Pops this my nigga D, D this my pops." Jayson says and the kid raises his head and I know who he is. I just nod my head looking at the double of a nigga I wanted to see in a grave, more than the pope wanted to see the pearly gates. However I kept my cool, because I had a game plan and when the smoke cleared I would be the last man standing. I grabbed a handful of chips from my sons bowl, nodded my head at them both. And made my way up stairs, I had a long day ahead of me.

Chapter 13: I'm only human

Lanya

It was my intentions of meeting up with Dinero before Alyssa's birthday party; however I had become so busy in my day to day, I let it slip. Add that to the fact that I was shaking with the thought of facing a man that I loved as if he were my blood, and he just turned on me. "Excuse me Ms. Marks your bags."

I turned to the woman behind the counter flashing my breath taking smile. I grabbed my packages with ease putting a little extra bounce in my step as I walked out of the pricey boutique. I walked up the block like I had not a care in the world, opening the door to my C-class. I pushed my sunglasses on the top of my head to hold my bangs in place as I started the car and dropped the top. Pulling out of the parking spot without even checking, I was just that confident in my skills.

I sped up the expressway; my long silky brown hair blew all over the place as I increased my speed. You couldn't tell me I didn't own the world. Pulling into my drive way as a steel gate opened and two armed guards stood on the outside of the gates like Kings Men. I knew I had to beef up security for the war that was about to start. Parking in my huge 6 car garage I grabbed my bags out of the back seat and proceeded into my 12,000 square foot home, in Bloomfield Hills, Michigan.

I dropped my bags at the entrance as I walked through my home I had fought so hard to keep. It was silent. Only the sound of my heels echoed in the house. I stood in the living room noticing a few things out of place. I'm not anal or anything, but I liked things a certain way.

"Marisa."

I yelled for the maid looking over my pictures on my fireplace.

"Yes Ms. Marks?"

The short older black woman with a Jamaican accent answered.

"My pictures who touched them?"

"The children had visitors and they looked at the photos ma'am."

"Visitor? Who? Where are my children?" I asked ready to hand her, her pink slip.

"Ma'am they are in their rooms."

I looked at Marisa with a snobby look then I sighed.

"Your dismissed Marisa. Thank you."

I proceeded up the stairs, my first stop was Alyssa's bedroom. Alyssa was 6 years old and was a perfect mixture of her father and I. Golden brown skin the color of light brown sugar. Her hair long and thick, always braided in one braid down the middle of her back. Her eyes almond shaped like a little china doll. Alyssa was very mature for her age. Despite the fact that she suffered from a life threatening illness.

"Hey Lyssa."

"Hey mommy, did you buy me anything?"

I smiled as I walked into her bedroom, lifting her into my arms.

"Wow aren't we nosey! Yes I bought you a few things and I will show them to you tomorrow! And why will you get them tomorrow?"

Alyssa gave me a huge smile.

"It's my birthday!"

My baby screamed tossing her arms in the air.

"Yes it is, you will be seven years old."

I sat Alyssa on her bed looking down at my wedding ring on my finger. A flash of me holding

Sacario's hand shot through my brain like a blazing bullet. A tear threatened to fall, but I ran my fingers under my eyes not allowing myself to be taken back to that place. My heart ached every time I thought about him or looked at our children. I kiss Alyssa and exit her room before I became emotional. Walking into Deuce's bedroom then stepping back out and tapping on the door before I entered.

"Come in mom," Deuce's deep voice says.

"Hey Sacario."

I smile looking at my baby boy. In my heart I know that he's not Sacario's son he and his sister barely look alike, but his actions say different. Deuce is Sacario's double and he is almost the spitting image of Dinero. From the light brown eyes to the creamy dark chocolate skin. His hair was thick with deep waves. And he was well over 6'0 feet and he was only 15. I just smiled admiring how handsome my son was.

"What's up ma?"

Deuce asked as he flopped down in his leather computer chair and leaned back looking up at me.

A smile filled my face as I picture Dinero and grined.

"Ma you there," he ask and I try and shake off the thought, but this time the tears fall.

I quickly wipe my tears and smile. I know that my son worries about me more than he should.

"Oh Marisa tells me we had company! Who was in our home and what business did they have looking at our photos?"

Deuce looked away like he had gone deaf.

"Sacario Lamar Al-,"

Pausing not finishing his last name. It was almost like it hurt to say that name.

"Sacario do you hear me?"

He rocked back and forth in his chair with a grin on his face.

"Man ma wasn't nobody up in here."

"Sacario watch your grammar and I'm sure that you had some fast tail little girl in my house, but I won't stress it!" I could smell the 212 cologne in the air. I knew only three men that made 212 smell like heaven on earth.

"Ma' you be trippin' damn!"

"Sacario I am your mother not your home girl, so watch yourself!" I say to my son annoyed with his tone.

"Sorry ma, but what'n no chick up in herre!"

All I could do is sigh as Deuce lied to my face. I shook my head and let out a dry laugh. "You are your father's son," I said turning to leave the room when I hear a smirk.

"Is that so?"

A deep voice echoed from behind me. I closed my eyes not wanting to turn around as a tear ran down my face. Deuce stood to his feet with a huge grin on his face as he moved past me rushing to his uncles.

"What up big man?"

Ali greeted his nephew with a dap and a side hug rubbing the top of his head looking into his glassy light brown eyes.

"What up sis?"

Dinero questioned in an even deeper voice reaching pass Ali, hugging Deuce.

"What are you doing here?"

"So we not welcomed? I thought we were family Nya." Dinero asked and I froze. Sacario, Ali and Dinero were my only true family, and I knew it however it was hard to get over the pain of abandonment I felt. When Sacario got locked up I counted on them to hold me down. I needed them to have my back, and they did whatever Sacario requested. I rolled my eyes and stepped in Dinero's face.

"I won't talk in front of my son! If you have something to say to me we can talk about it downstairs!"

I pushed past both men turning back looking at my son with hurt in my eyes.

"Sacario if you think for a second that I didn't know that they were here, you are as dumb as your father as well."

I grit my teeth walking down to my bedroom slamming the door. Finally I could exhale thinking of the words I had just said to Deuce. I kicked off my heels then my dress. I walked around my bedroom in just my panties, a part of me wanted Ali to come in my room and toss me to the bed. I walked into my bathroom and turned on the shower. Pulling my hair into a ponytail; then I leaned over the sink and looked in the mirror. After all these years a part of me was still very insecure.

'Don't do this to yourself! You have come too far to let them come in your life and make you doubt yourself!' I sighed just thinking that I wasn't even fooling myself. Biting down on my bottom lip sitting on the edge of the tub, I let the tears that I had been holding fall down my face.

"Damn you, damn you Sacario, you told me that you would protect me! That I was yours! So where the fuck are you!? Ahhhhhhhh, I hate you for leaving me!"

I yelled in anger picking the first thing my hands could rest on and tossing it.

"You gone hurt somebody with that." A voice said, I couldn't make out the face just the shadow image that sat on my bed. I exhaled and stood walking into my bedroom a slight smile on my face. Knowing that Ali and I were going to cross the line this time for sure. I covered my breast as we moved towards each other. Before I could go any further my heart stopped. I froze, I felt as if all the breath had left my body.

"You can't be here! They locked you away! How – ?"

"I have guards and you can't,,," I cried unable to finish any statements, as I looked at a face I prayed to

Jesus I would never see again. I wanted to scream as he pulled me into his arms and kissed my neck.

"Ummm baby girl you smell just like I remember and feel even better." He pushed my legs apart never letting my waist go and kissed my neck. I could feel his stiffness and my skin crawled.

"Keith don't do this."

I begged through grit teeth.

"Why not baby girl? You love it when I fuck you! Don't you like it when daddy fucks you, tell me you love daddy's dick." He said in my ear and I cried.

"No I don't and my brother-in-laws are both in there and they will kill you with no question!" I said with confidence pulling away from Keith. However I felt like a small child. I was the insecure little fourteen year old that I worked so hard to shake.

"Then our son will get a video tape telling him who his real father is! Do you want your perfect son to know that the only father he knows is not his daddy .Do you truly want him to know that he's not who he thinks he is!?" Keith says smiling.

"You wouldn't!"

"If you think I won't try me! If I don't come out of this house by 10 pm tonight my watch out will go to the cops and tell them everything. Then they will hand deliver Jr. a very visual confession! You know all those night you use to sit on your knees and drink from my spout and I would run my fingers through your hair!" I closed my eyes tightly wanting to die from the words he said. Deuce was Sacario's, he could never know about my past, hell Sacario could never know that Deuce was a product of a man raping me. I had kept that secret for sixteen years and I planned on it going to the grave with me. I allowed him to pull me back into his space. I bit down on my bottom lip as he ran his hands through my hair, and then he removed my panties. I could feel his fingers and he pushed them inside of me. The pain was almost unbearable, I hadn't been penetrated since Sacario had last made love to me. that was over seven years. I gritted my teeth tightly wanting to scream.

"Damn baby girl that shit as tight as our first time."

A tear rolled down my face as a tap on the door forced Keith to retract his fingers.

"Say anything and my protégé will sneak in that pretty little girl's room every night you'll never sleep. Answer the door."

I looked back at Keith hating him more in that second. I wanted to run to whoever stood on the other side and tell them the truth, however I couldn't risk that what he said he would truly do. I grabbed my robe from behind the door and stepped out the room shutting the door behind me.

Ali stood before me looking as tasty as he had always looked. He was the color of milk chocolate and every bit as smooth; standing at 6 feet 5 inches and 300 pounds of pure man. He spoke educated slang and didn't mind that he wasn't as hard as his brothers, his cocky swag spoke for itself. "Hey Nya can we talk?" Ali asked and I felt numb.

"My name is Lanya and I'm busy Ali! So can we talk later?" I say my body shaking.

"One, yo name is what yo husband call you and that's Nya; two naw this about Sacario and his money!"

"What about his money? Y'all took everything from me the bars, the barbershop, the cars, the houses, you left me with nothing when I made sure y'all had it all!"

"Nya that's bullshit and you know it!"

He moved the falling hair out of my face and tried to peep in her room, when I tightened the door he allowed his eyes to settle on my perfect thick body. He had a light smile over his face as he tried to look away.

"Nya we tried to give you money and take care of you, but you turned away! You divorced my brother and even tried selling on our turf and all that was looked over."

"Your brother turned his back on us, his family. I almost died trying to bring his daughter in the world. I watched them gun his baby brother down! I won't do this Ali, not with you, I owe you nothing. If you will excuse me I have a shower to take!"

Not giving Ali a chance to speak I slammed the door leaving him on the other side. I exhaled and leaned up against the door. Forgetting that Keith was there.

"Oh baby girl come her! Let daddy make you feel better."

I bit down on my bottom lip trying not to cry. Falling to the floor hating what was coming next.   Keith lifted my body and barley moving he undressed me. I wanted to fight, but I couldn't I just mumbled no as he stroked his dick and penetrated me. Why was he doing this I cried to myself, but I knew the reason control, and power. Once again a man had made me a victim. I can't continue like this I thought to myself as I lie in my bed watching him dress, and vanish.

Chapter 14: Blood brothers

Ali

They say you can't move forward, till you look behind you. For some reason my past was hunting me and truthfully I didn't know why. I thought maybe because yet again I had let myself fall for the wrong woman. I don't know what it is about Lanya that gets me so fired up. However I want lie my brother's wife gives me chills. I sat my car seat back trying to get Lanya out my head. The last two encounters we had, the thoughts alone were enough for my brother to kill me. I had to laugh, MY BROTHER I thought to myself. Sacario had been my brother since day one. A smile covered my face as I let my mind drift to my past...

The past...

I met Dinero and Sacario when I was seven years old. We all stayed in the same group home waiting, for either a foster home or some sad sap to give us a once over and adopt us. However at seven I was no fool, I truly didn't think anyone would want a child of a crack head. And that is what my mother was, a Crack whore fuckin with her supplier who knocked her up and six years later, was the cause of her death. I won't lie a part of me will always hate both my parents; crazy that hate for my parents is what brought my brothers and I together. We both hated our parents for leaving us abruptly. Never did we imagine that we were, all the sons of the biggest cocaine supplier in Michigan. However a bond of brothers didn't come from the blood we shared, but the trust we put in each other at an early age. Right away Dinero and I clicked. However Sacario had always been shy and standoffish. It wasn't until they sent Dinero to a group home for children ten and over, did Sacario feel the need to act out. I never understood why he felt the need to be a problem child when he was always so quiet. However one night he messed with the wrong kid, snatched the food right off his tray. What Sacario didn't know was this boy had like four friends ready to rip into him. They would have killed him; he was only seven and the skinniest kid I had ever seen in life. I knew they would rip him to shreds so I protected him, from that day forward we were best friends. I was adopted at thirteen by a former Navy officer and his wife, they wanted Sacario as well but he felt like if he left Dinero would never be able to find him so he acted out, making him ineligible for adoption. However that didn't stop him from being my number one nigga. Whatever Sacario did I was a part of it from hustling, to stealing cars, even when he got hooked up with that nigga Silk. I begged him not to trust niggas from a past he knew nothing about, but he was dumb to my words. He assures me he would be fine, and that was the first time in ten years we separated when I went away College. That was the one time he needed me and I wasn't there. That was my vow; that would be the last time I didn't have his six.

Present day

A tap on my window pulls me from my thoughts, I realize as I hit the unlock switch that once again I had failed my number one. I started my engine looking to my passenger and pulled off. Guilt heavy on my heart I pulled a blunt from the ashtray pushed my car lighter in and slid the blunt between my lips. I lit the blunt took two pulls and passed it. Still in a bit of a daze as I drove

The ride to my crib was long and silent the only thing shared between myself and my passenger were the three blunts.

I pulled in my drive way put my car in park and hopped out I couldn't wait to get inside I pulled my key and made it to the door when a hand touched my shoulder. I paused turning to look at my best friend, my brother tears in my eyes as he pulled me to him and hugged me.

"My nigga, what don't kill me made me," he said and we walk into the house.

Chapter 15   Tears of Pain

Lanya

I looked down at my wedding ring once again wanting to take them off. I was so mad that after seven years he was still the first thing on my mind. I shook his images from my mind and started to stir the pot in front of me. "Deuce I yell as I hear my son run down the stairs. He walks into the kitchen fully dressed. My son is so handsome, and every time I see him, I think of Dinero because of his rich chocolate color.

"What up ma?" He asked kissing my face and grabbing a slice of bacon from the plate.

"Duce I need yo help with the party today it will be a lot of people here and I can't do it alone" I tell him referring to my daughter's birthday party. His phone began to ring for the third time since, he has been before me I shoot him a look. He nods his head press talk on his phone and walks away. The sound of the doorbell, made me jump. I turned off the stove wiped my hands and walked into the living room. Saint stood at my door with a clip board and a package. .

"Morning Mrs. Alton this package was left at the gate, and this is the guest list that I need you to ok."

I smiled and even blushed as the smell of green jolly ranchers and weed invades my nose. Saint licked his lips ; I took the packages and flashed Saint a smile.

"Sean you know my name is Marks. But you can call me Lanya! With ya cute little self."

"Thanks Mrs. Alton but I have my orders."

He took the clip board and handed me the huge gift wrapped, in birthday wrapping paper. I took the package and watched as Saint exited. Putting the box to my ear then giving it a little shake as I sat it down going back to my preparation.

"Is that mine mommy?" Alyssa asked I smiled and kissed my baby girls fore head taking her hand I guided her up the stairs. Alyssa was extremely excited as she skipped upstairs into her bedroom. I wished I could share in her joy; however my mind was all over the place. The encounter with Keith had my mind off track. In addition to the thoughts I had been having about Ali I was confused. I watched as my daughter pulled out her pink fluffy dress and matching Gucci shoes. My daughter was her father's child as she laid out ever article of clothes before going into the bathroom. I plopped down on her bed and let my mind drift. Wishing that my...

I had to catch myself from thinking of Sacario as my husband. A tear fell down my eye just as my phone began to ring.

I reached in my pocket and pulled my phone wiping my face and clearing my throat before I answered.

"Hello"

"Why you sound so sad," a deep sexy voice said. The voice gave me chills I knew I had heard it before however I knew it wasn't Sacario or any of his brothers. I looked at my phone and the number was unregistered so I hesitated to answer.

"Lanya you there?" He questioned with concern

"Yes" I said in a whisper still trying to fill him out.

"This Jayce in case you sitting trying to figure it out,"

"Jayce," I mouthed then it hit me the dude from my uncle's bar in flint. I tried to fight the smile, however it was too late as I stood from Lyssa's bed and walked out of her room. I walked down to my room and lightly closed my door before I spoke another word.

"You there?" He asked and I eagerly answered yes.

"Well I know you're a busy woman, but I was hoping that maybe you would allow me to take you for drinks tonight," I bit down on my bottom lip and scaled the room.

"Drinks, tonight? I can't,...

"Why is that? he said stopping me in midsentence.

"Today is my daughter's birthday—

"Say no more" He cut me off again this time I could hear a cocky smirk in his tone.

"Well can I have a rain check" I asked smiling from ear to ear.

"I'd have it no other way, talk to you later sexy" He said in a sexy swag and ended the call leaving a smile on my face. I hadn't even noticed that my daughter had walked into the bedroom dressed and spinning around so I can take a look. I smiled at my baby springing to my feet to embrace her.

≈ ≈ ≈ ≈ ≈ ≈

It took hours, but finally guest had arrived and the party was off to a great start. I stood alone in my huge back yard admiring my handy work. Alyssa's party truly looked like a world class events from the women dressed as princess greeting guest, the three bounce house, carriage and train rides. I loved big events and was so pleased that I could do it for my daughter. The smile on her face could make any bad day good I thought to myself as I looked up and watched as Kym, my former best friend walked in with Dinero in tow, he held their two year old son that I had yet to meet. I couldn't believe that these people were at my home, and didn't bother to speak to me as they hugged and kissed my children. I felt anger creep over me; finally I took a deep breath and looked down at the wedding ring that still sat on my finger and twisted it, fighting the tears that sat in my eyes. I never missed him more than I did in that one moment.

"Damn that nigga must be the shit if you rocking his ring" That voice invaded my mind. My body shook as I blocked it out of my head. No way could it be him I thought to myself. I slowly turned to see Sacario towering over me. He hadn't changed much, of course his arms were the size of Popeye the sailor man, but his sexy peanut butter colored skin, full lips and gorgeous golden brown eyes that every Alton man seem to have. A spark shot through my body as I leaped into his arms a million pounds off my shoulder as we both tumbled to the ground. He laid on his back and pull me to him his lips touched mine for the first time in seven years and tears a smile filled my face. I pulled away to look at him, and in that second I realized I hated him. I raised my hand and smacked him as hard as I could before I pulled myself from the ground and running into my house.

Sacario

A sight for score eyes would be an understatement, I thought as I watched my wife leaned against a huge tree in a long flowing sundress. I had missed her more than anything in this world. I just hoped she would receive me well, However the smack, I got I really didn't see coming.

I chased her into the house that I was totally unfamiliar with. She ran up the spiraled stair case and I was right behind her taking four stairs at a time. She tried to slam the door in my face but I slid my size 13 timberland in the door and forced my way in. She ran to the other side of the room like she feared me and slid to the floor holding herself.

"Fuck wrong wit you?" I asked her walking over to her and snatching her up and pressing her against the wall. I stared into her eyes, and wiped the tears that were falling.

"Baby you not happy to see me?" She shook her head uncontrollably before she dropped her head on my chest and just began to cry. I lifted her chin and planted a passionate kiss on her lips she smiled and dropped her face back to my chest.

"Nya I love you baby" I say in her ear and she lifts her head almost like I struck a nerve. She pushes her self away from me and crosses her arms over her, still perfect perky breast. I lick my lips looking at my babe with her bottom lip in her mouth and that ice glare in her eyes.

"Say something mama" I say to her pulling her back to me and she smacks my hand.

"Fuck you Sacario, Fuck you! She turns her back to me and I snap.

Snatching her back up

"Watch yo tone with me I'm not one of these niggas on the street I'm yo husband

"You sure bout that KILLA?" She spit my street name out like venom.

"Fuck u mean am I sure? Hell yeah!"

Hum well state of Michigan say were divorced, and right now is not the time to talk about it, it's my daughter's birthday and I'm off to enjoy her party. She didn't give me a chance to response before she was walking out the door.

≈ ≈ ≈ ≈ ≈ ≈

I stood outside with my brothers watching all these kids run by wondering which one was my daughter. I hadn't seen her since she was a baby, and although her mother made sure to send me family pictures it tore me up too look at my family without me.

"Sup Kid?" Ali ask standing beside me he point at my daughter, I couldn't help but laugh that nigga had been reading my mind since we were kids.

"Lyssa, Lyssa Nya yells and the pretty little girl with long hair and grey eyes runs right pass me she looks up at Ali and smile as she makes her way over to her mother. I look at my son who is the spitting image of Ali, He lifts her in to a chair in front of a table full of gifts. I want to join them, however I keep my distance and it kills me.

Dinero joins us as I watch my wife walk into the house.

"Man fuck that bitch, she couldn't even do a bid," Dinero blankly says and I shoot him a side eye and look back at my daughters smile. She gorgeous even though she looks nothing like myself or her mother. Lanya walks out the house with a large gift and place in front of my daughter, I smile as she rips into the box with no mercy, however my heart drops when my daughter starts to scream. I run to her my brothers on my heels, that nigga Saint walks off his post his gun in his hand, when my Son Lifts his sister into his arms and holds her body tightly.

Ali

Dinero stood in Lanya's living room looking into the gift box shaking his head. He lifted his head looking at Lanya then Sacario and myself.

"Sacario take your sister upstairs baby" Nya huffs

BRUNSWICK

"No Nya I want to see her" Sacario begs Nya and a part of me wants to smack them both

Lanya gave Sacario a hard looked then looked at her son.

"Duce do as I said!"

"Ma but she wants to see him!" I laugh as my nephew raises his voice

Lanya stumped her foot and looked at both Deuce and my brother.

"Deuce I don't care do as I said now I am your mother!"

"And I'm there father or did you forget! Sacario said

"Yeah she forgot!"

Dinero blurted out. As he sucked his teeth at Lanya. Lanya rolled her eyes back and sucked her teeth.

"No I didn't forget shit Sacario! Those are your children and I have not denied them of that! But they don't need to be down here when Dinero got that look in his eye and Ali rubbing his badge like he a real cop! Crooked motherfucka!"

I sucked my teeth and looked at Lanya out the corner of my eye sick of her mouth ., her judgment. I walked over to her grabbing her arm pushing her against the wall.

"This crooked motherfucka saved your husband ass and brought him back to you!"

I tighten my grip and looked in her eyes. As they watered

"Hear me one time Nya these are my brothers we didn't turn our back on you! You took the word of yo bitch ass niggas and walked out on yo family so don't you dare."

Sacario grabbed me walking me over to the box. We all looked in the box. Only Dinero was brave enough to touch it as Sacario closed his eyes and lost his footing. Lanya stood behind him her hand in his back holding him up

"Who is it Cari?" She questioned him, like she was concerned. As if she hadn't just been yelling in his face. I sucked my teeth laughing to myself confirming how Bipolar this bitch really was.

Sacario grabbed his wife and pulled her close not letting her look in the box.

"It was just an arm an eye ball and a sheet of paper that said eye for an eye. Your next!"

Lanya screamed and held her head into Sacario's chest.

"Get it out of here! Please baby get it out she cried in his arms.

I took out my phone calling SaintI moved quickly handing Saint the box.

"Don't open it just get rid of it!"

Sacario frowned as I entered back in the room!

"You just made him get rid of his brother's body parts!" Dinero laughed at the thought of Saint tossing Justice's frozen body parts

"I had no choice I need his head clear for this job."

Sacario looked at his wife with a slight smile; then nodded his head.

Lanya looked at him nodded back she rolled her eyes and started up the stairs, it was as if he gave her an order without his mouth opening.

"Alright Lee what the fuck we gone do?"

Sacario questioned me. We all took a seat in Lanya's living room discussing who we thought would do something so hateful as I cut a body part from a man that had been dead for years and gift wrap it for a child to open. To Dinero it was no question Dice and Smooth Marks could only do something so devise. An eye for an eye Sacario and Dinero repeated in unison.

It was clear we were all thinking back to how they beheaded Silk and delivered him to his wife's door step.

We need a trip Sacario how soon before you can leave the state?"

Dinero questioned with a light bulb in his head.

"He got at least three months before he should make any moves and they still gone be watching." I quickly answered seeing that Sacario was ready to move.

"That's cool because I need to get reacquainted with my family!" Killa said and I shot Dinero a look

"Why would you want that bitch?"

Dinero questioned and I had to second that.

Sacario smiled and looked at us like no words had to be said. He cleared his throat and smiled a greedy smile.

"Yo because y'all my brothers I will say this one time and its over! Just not here let's hit the Bosses Lounge I need a drink."

We all walked out the door. Sacario paused turning to walking back in the house.

Sacario

Just as I was about to walk out the door I knew that I had to let my wife know what was going on. I couldn't leave her like I did years ago. I ran upstairs into her bedroom to find her in tears. I sat beside her stroking her cheek wiping the tears away in one swoop.

"Cario how did we get like this?" She asked and I wanted to tell her everything I did was for a reason. I needed to tell her it was all to protect her. I couldn't risk the Feds or none of them Alphabet niggas coming in and dragging her away. Destroying my family so I did what I needed to do for her, for Deuce and my daughter. I knew it would hurt her, but not more than I would hurt being locked up and knowing that my family had nothing. Nya was a great woman and I won't lie I wanted to lay next to her in that bed and give her what I thirsted for, for years, but she was a werk and my mind was on something else.

I looked down at my cell phone, as it vibrated and so did Nya.

"So someone has your number, but not your so called wife." I looked at Olivia's name and number and laughed.

"Man it's just Lee," I leaned in to kiss her face and she turned her head.

"Nya did you mean anything you said in those 1000's of letters you sent?" I asked and she turned her whole body. My phone rang again and she quickly turned to see who it was.

"Baby I'm stay with my brothers give you a chance to get use to me being out I'll come by tomorrow and see you and the kids. I kissed her face not giving her a chance to reply. I stood from the bed and walked down stairs. I haft way expected her to chase me, but she didn't so I just made my way out the door Lanya still heavy on mind.

Chapter 16: Mistakes and regrets

Kym

I sat in the middle of my bed painting my toe nails. I can't get Nya off my mind we had been best friends since we were little kids and now we don't even speak. I won't lie I miss the fuck out of her, but Nero said she turned her back on them so what am I to do. I mean Dinero has done so much for me and I can't go against him. However I know that were it not for Nya I would never even be with him. God I feel so guilty, but she had her chance to be with a boss nigga and she walked away. I tell myself, every day to ease the guilt.

"Damn ma you like wine, you get better wit time." A deep voice says causing me to jump out my skin spilling the lime green nail polish on my bed. I look up to see a face that I hadn't seen in years. A face that, I loved and feared at the same time.

"Twan what are you doing here?" I question my ex-boyfriend. Twan was Daylin's best friend and the first man I called myself loving. That is until he got me hooked on coke, and had me tricking just to get a fix. It came to a point where I got so high I would forget days. It took Twan getting locked up, for me to kick the bad habit.

"Damn baby you act like you not happy to see me," he says licking his lips and bending to touch my leg. A chill shot down my spine and I didn't know rather to scream or cry. Twan had the ability to make me weak. After all he was sexy as hell his midnight blacks skin big brown eyes full lips and long braids. His body was nothing to ignore, and the fact he had just done a bid um um um. I have said it once and I will say it again jail dose a body good.

I jumped back and walked to the other side of the room.

"Twan how you get in here?" I asked as my phone began to ring. Twan smiled as I reached to the night stand pressing talk. My heart was racing I didn't even realize I was out of breath until I could barely say hello.

"Fuck you doing?" Dinero yelled through the phone

"Nothing baby, I mean I was cleaning up changing the sheets washing clothes stuff like that," I say glancing back up not to see Twan, then I felt his arms around my waist and my body shook.

"Oh Ok How Shawn doing?" he asked about our son and I couldn't even think how to speak, all I kept thinking is if O come home and find this man here. I don't even want to think what he will do to me.

"Kym!" Dinero yelled and I jump out my thoughts.

"I'm sorry babe you know how I am when I'm cleaning the house. I like things to be done right." He laughs and a bit of stress rolls off my back as Twan runs his hands down my jogging pants and kisses my neck.

"Alight don't do too much babe I will home in about 20 minutes just gone stop get some Thai food and some movies. My heart really starts to jump out my chest as I end the call without even saying good bye.

"You have to go Twan I say pulling away. He grabs my arm and tosses me to the bed, ripping my legs apart he stands between them and bend to kiss my neck.

"You gone rape me Twan?" I ask in a loud tone. I push him back to see my baby standing in my bedroom with his bottle in his hand. Could this day get any worse? I think to myself; rushing to take my son into his room. I lay him in his bed and kiss his face. I assure him I will be back and I go back to see Twan standing in my room with a smile on his face.

"So that's how that ass got so fat you got a son." He said and I roll my eyes.

"Look ma I'm not gone fuck up yo good thing, you just owe me mama."

"Owe you! What the fuck could I owe you? Nigga you...," he placed his hand over my mouth to shut me up, because I was ready to tell him about himself.

"Bitch if it was not for me you wouldn't have shit! I gave you life!" He says sucking his teeth and pulling a gun from his waist band.

"Look bitch, I don't want beef with yo man, not yet atleast but I do know that nigga got a stash here, and if you don't want him to come home and find me fuckin the dog shit out you and a bullet in his seed..," I put my finger in my ears when he said he would kill JayShawn I rushed to the closet and unlocked Dinero's safe. My hands poured sweat and I wanted to cry as I pulled the two bricks of coke Nero kept. I really had no time to think of what Dinero would do to me, or the lie I would have to tell to get out of the coke being missing, all I knew was that I needed this man out my house.

"Take it" I said slamming the coke into his chest. He smiled and went into kiss me. I turned my head and he dropped the coke to the ground and grabbed my face.

"See you think cuz this nigga fucking you and you sucking him, you his. But Bitch you mine and always, will be. The reason you fuck him and suck him so good cuz I taught you how to take the dick. Now you can keep playing games if you want and I can show you better than I can tell you." He bent in kissing my lips, pushed me backwards and kissed my face. I blinked my eyes and when I opened them Twan was gone. I could barely get to my feet before I heard the door slam and heard heavy foot steps up the stairs.

Dinero

Kym's voice was shaky on the phone. I knew she was lying about something so I said fuck picking up a movie we could do Netflix. I grabbed the food and made it through the door to hear my son crying. I ran upstairs to his room picked him up and walked in the room where my girl was sitting on her knees like she was praying.

"Sup babe" I say and she damn near has a heart attack.

"Fuck wrong wit you today. I look at the house looking like I left it with the exception of nail polish spilt on the bed.

"Nothing baby I just was praying" she said walking to kiss me and I turn my head.

I sit my son on the floor knowing this bitch is a hoe in that second. I place my hands around her throat and stare in her eyes. I don't press her neck hard, but she knows I want to kill her so she starts the water works.

"Tell me now Kym," I order and release her neck. She picks are son up and walks him into his room I stay on her heels as she tries to close the door in my face.

I push the door in and she holds my son in the air as a shield.

"Let me lay him down Nero please?" I nod my head and she lays Shawn down kisses his face and walks out the room.

I grab her arm ready to kill her ass.

"I miss Nya O, I'm depressed and alone and starting to hate you, because I have no one, but you and you never here. She wraps her arms around my waist and I feel the guilt I pick her up and kiss her lips walking her down to the bedroom. I toss her to the bed and drop to my knees kissing her stomach as I slide her jogging pants off her. She runs her hand over my head and I wonder how much of it was true and a lie, but I will know in seconds, because I know my pussy. From the way it taste, smell and feel. I slip my finger in her hole and she a little wet, I place my lips on her clit and began to suck and she starts to moan. I laugh, as I run my tongue over her clit. Biting down as I slide two fingers in her pussy. She starts to move her hips as I give her the business. My dick is hard as bricks so I pull my jeans down, lift Kym from the bed and slide my whole pipe in, loving the shocked look she always gets. Her moans drive me crazy, and I feel her warm juices run down my dick.

"Yeah this my shit I tell her knowing it's just how I left it. I pound harder and harder bringing her to tears, and me to a nut. I fall to the bed and her beside me I kiss her lips.

"Call yo girl tomorrow, tonight you spend with yo man.

Chapter 17: Love and Loyalty...

ALI

My brother had been staying with me for the past month, and I watched him fuck with numerous hoes, none like Nya. He had to know that Nya was the best he would ever get, however the bitch that stood out was the lawyer chick Olivia. She had spent the night and I'm sure that's who he had been spending his spare time with. I wasn't jealous, however I'm not gone front like I didn't think my brother was fucking up.

"Hey unk," my nephew says walking into my house and flopping on the sofa across from me.

"What up nephew?" Looking at my double. Deuce always reminded me of a mixture of the three of us it was crazy to me.

you here to see yo pops?" I asked him as he skims down his phone.

"Man He called me over her, cause him and ma Beefing I guess," He said, and I couldn't help but laugh as the bitch Olivia walks down the stairs and walks over to me kissing my cheek.

"Damn unk" Duece said admiring Olivia

"Hey brother; how are you?" She said looking dead at my nephew.

"You must be little Sacario, you look just like...." she paused and looked at me and smiled.

Deuce stood and gave me a side eye as he extends his hand to Olivia.

"I'm Deuce, you are?"

"Babe you...." Sacario pauses when he sees his son looking at him like he sick.

"What's up D?" He says to his son walking over to him and hugging him.

"Yo mom with you?" Sacario ask as he walks away from Deuce and sits on the couch, Olivia follows sitting on his lap.

Deuce shakes his head and smiles.

"Naw pops, mom at home crying every night cause you haven't been home."

I shake my head and standup giving Deuce and Killa a chance to talk that shit out, but I'm not gone act like I wasn't thinking the same thing. I grab my keys and my phone head out the house. My thought was to head to Nya house instead I hit a little strip club, paid for VIP and made myself comfortable. I was expecting a hoe to come give me a dance, but not a pussy to come begging for handouts. Little nigga I hadn't seen in years flops down and waves a waitress over. I pull my gun from my waist and place it on my lap. Perks of having a badge, I had no problem having my gun where other niggas couldn't.

"Yo Big Lee I thought that was you!" I smirked and looked the nigga over. The waitress cames and sat a drink in front of me and ask that nigga what he drinking.

"He won't be here long enough for drinks," I said and he smiles.

"Rum and coke ma"

"Nah dead that shit," I order tossing the waitress a bill and sending her on her way.

"Yo Boss why it got to be like that? I'm just trying to be put on, son. He say like he been in New York and I know off rip he can't be trusted.

"Put on wit what" I ask and he smile nigga Twan thought I didn't know who he was, but I should have sent Saint to body his ass when I heard he was out. I sucked my teeth and took another drink looking at this wack nigga.

"You know boss just need a little help, I'm just getting out the joint—

I cut himoff right there My Nigga we good and all, but what you talking bout I can't help you with I stood from the booth tossing another bill and walked off.

Sacario

I sat looking at my phone, wanting to dial my wife's number, but I truly didn't know what my son had told her. Just as I sat my phone on the night table and cut the lights off my phone lit up. I half way wanted it to be my wife, but of course it was Olivia, I pressed ignore, for it to light up again.

"What?" I shouted into the phone annoyed that this shit started as just business and she wanted more than I was willing to give.

"Pops," my son says catching me off guard.

"What's up D?"

"Pops I just got home and ma here crying, its men in our house you want me to handle this shit!" He asks and I hop out the bed.

"Nah nigga go in yo room I'm on my way." I tell him ending the call and slip into some jogging pants and my Jays. Don't even bother to put on a shit, my wife beater will have to do as I reach in my night stand grab the burner and tuck it in my waist grab an extra clip snatch up my phone and rush out the door.

I dial Lee as I pull out the driveway, but as I pull out he's pulling in. I hope out my ride and wave for him to follow me. I jump back in the car and start to text Nero wondering what the fuck is going on. In that minute I knew it was time to go home.

~ ~ ~

I make it to my wife's spot and Saint is on his post. I stop my car and roll the window down

"Who in my house?"

"Mrs. Alton brought home guest." He tells me and I drive in Ali behind me. I park my truck and hop out pulling my burner as Ali gets out his car.

"Nigga put that shit up!" He yells and I'm sure he dumb as fuck, but I tuck my gun in my waist band and run up to the front door. I have keys because my son made sure of that. However I knock on the door. No one answers the first two minutes so I try the door, and it's unlocked so I walk in.

"Nya?" I say looking to my left to see two big black niggas sitting on my couch like they live here. Nya is walking down the stairs in a short ass T shirt carrying a duffle bag. She sees me and turns to walk back upstairs, I catch a glimpse of her ass poking out no panties. This bitch must want to die, I think to myself.

"Get the fuck down here." I order her my gun now in my hand and I look over at my brother who is now stroking his gun.

Lanya looks away then she runs to me.

"What Cari?"

"Fuck you doing round my kids?" I snatch the bag from her hand and she lunges at me. I grab her midair and toss her to the floor. I unzip the duffle bag to see stacks of cash. I look over at the dudes sitting like they own my shit and I cock my gun.

"Fuck y'all need with my wife?"

Lanya jumps up and gets in my face. I push her back but she crying so I toss Lee the bag and lift her in the air.

"Who are you giving my money to?"

"Let me go Cari its not yo fuckin money, I work for everything I got Sacario." The men stand to leave and Ali cuts them off and Lanya cries harder.

"Stop it Lee let them go, don't do this."

"You fucking other niggas Nya?"

"Why you care nigga you fucking other hoes," she say. Barking on me and I drop her to the ground.

"Man Nya you pissing me off."

"Now you know how I feel," she yells and I push her towards the stairs. She pulls away walks over to Lee snatches the bag and hand it to the older dude.

"Keith just go."

Ali grabs him and she push Lee.

"This is my house, my life Cario. You and yo fuckin brother need to go." She yells like a mad woman.

"You are my fuckin wife." She looks at me with tears in her eyes and she starts to swing her hands in my face.

"Yo wife that you left, you left me. Not when you went to jail, when you sent that bitch to my house and took my name, my home and everything you assured me was mine. Then you smile in my fuckin face as soon as you get out and go to your brothers for a fuckin month. What you think I'm deaf, dumb and stupid Sacario?

Either you gay as fuck from years in jail, or you fuck other hoes because you have been nowhere near this pussy." I didn't know if it was the gay remark or the fact she was in my face, I flipped and knocked her to the ground. I stood over her in rage ready to murder her when Lee grabbed my shoulder.

"That's yo wife!" My brother tells me as I look down at my wife and she covering her whole body, I look behind me and the two dudes are gone, and on the stairs stand my son. I bend down to help Nya up and she smacks my hand. I grab her off the floor and lift her to me and Ali shakes his head.

"Let's go bro," Lanya pushes me and Ali grabs her and pull her upstairs. My son turns and follows behind them. In that moment I didn't know if I felt more shame for putting my hands on my wife, or the fact that my son had seen me do so.

Ali

The thing about Alton men is; we are kings. What we do should not be repeated by women. I didn't condone the fact that my brother fucked around on his wife. Hell I thought that was a huge mistake. Lanya was a rare type of woman, one that he had molded from scratch, she was the type of woman that I would love to have, in fact I was sure that Dinero felt the same as I did. However she knew better than to fuck around on, him.

Ring or no ring Nya was an Alton and Loyalty is all that we will accept. So I knew when we walked in that house and she was exposed my brother was gone to lose his mind. I expected a blood bath that of course I would have to fix, so the way that Killa handled it I had to give him his props. Nevertheless I couldn't let him kill his wife in front of my nephew. I grabbed Nya up and took her into her bed room. Fear covered her face and her body shook as I slammed the door.

"Who was that man? I asked her trying to keep my sanity. She turned her head, and I grabbed her face forcing her to look at me. Lanya who the fuck was that nigga, why the fuck would you allow Deuce to see you like that. She started to laugh and pushed me off her. "Why the fuck you care who around, my son Ali."

"Because he my—I paused watching as Lanya walked away and began to dress I noticed the bruises on the back of her leg, I wanted to protect her so badly, but from what. "Ali you are not my man, just like Killa is not my husband. Deuce is neither of your concern—

She said causing me to snap I grabbed her and tossed her to the wall. Lanya gave me a blank stare like she didn't even fear death. "What Lee you worried that your brother gone put two and two together and realize that the reason his son looks more like you, then he looks like him, is because you fucked me? Shhh Lee I won't tell." She mocked me and pushed away. I had only wondered if Deuce was mine one time. That was the reason I named him Deuce, because he was someone's second. However I put it out my head knowing that Nya was already pregnant when she started working at the bar, and if I had knew she had fucked my brother I would have never— She started to cry pulling me from my thoughts.

"Nya you know D is not my son.

"But he should be, Why shouldn't – the door opened causing Lanya to freeze in her words.

"I miss something?" Sacario says and I look to Lanya to tell him the situation.

"No Killa, everything is peachy!" Lanya says walking towards the bath room, Sacario moved quickly and grabbed her. He tossed her to the wall, and I'm sure he broke something the way it sounded when she hit the wall. "This shit is old, Lanya you are my fuckin wife these are my kids—Sacario paused and looked at me. He let off a slight smile and focused back on his wife. You not a kid no more you got grow the fuck up. This how we doing it from now I'm coming home, shit you doing is over! You understand" She dropped her head and started to whimper then again that stare appeared on her face as she lifted her head.

"Fuck you Killa! You been out for how long? No time been spent in this home, that's one. Two this is my shit I got it without you so I damn sure can manage it just fine the same way." She pushed him backwards and began to walk away. This is my house, these are my kids. This is my pussy, who I fuck suck love and want is no longer of yo concern. I can't believe I loved you. She said walking towards the bathroom again. I just knew that my brother was gone lose it, but he nodded his head and nodded for me to exit as he lead the way.

Chapter 18: KILLA

Sacario

Clearly I had been away way to long and people were starting to forget who the hell I was and why the fuck they called me Killa. My first thought was to fight for my wife. Fuck that shit I had done that too many times. Lanya was mine, not worried about her going nowhere. I know her Bi polar ass would be right back, on my dick in a matter of seconds. I was more worried about the street and what I was hearing. From my understanding my wife had left a hellfire mess for me to clean. Starting with the fact that her bum ass uncles; couldn't take me head on so they called for the one nigga that I should have taken out years ago. Did they think that Money Santa was really that nigga on the street cuz he did a few things in Flint. Nah not at all. Money was a fuckin follower that would never have shit on me. I knew that nigga since I was 16 and we was both runners for the nigga Silk. He was supposed to be the nigga that take the game when Silk met his maker, however it was clear to Silk and Money that I was a better choice, that's why they came up with the plan to set me up and rob me for all my work. Were it not for Dinero, Yeah my life would have come to an abrupt end! That's why it was so clear that I was supposed to be king. That's why it was no sweat off my back to end Silk and send his body parts to, not only his wife, but his hoe. It was no stress to me to hire his son to take out his entire blood, line. And when I fell for his only daughter, I created a blood line that consisted of both families. So why the Marks brothers thought that, a wack ass nigga like Money could take out a nigga like me. I was a fuckin mastermind, not too much that could take me out. However I would be the death of this nigga. Normally I would, just let Saint take this nigga out, but death would be too good for this nigga. Not only did this nigga set me up, he also was responsible for putting crack in my sons hand. I knew that Deuce would follow in my footsteps, however I refuse to allow another man give him the game, for that alone I would make sure Jayce Money Santa died nice and slow. "What's on yo mind bro?" Dinero asked pulling me from my thoughts. He passes me the blunt that he had just lit.

"Shit bro, Murder" I told Dinero and he nodded as we sat in my Truck blazing a blunt and keeping a close eye on the nigga money. We had followed this nigga three nights in a row watching how he ran his crew. The Take Money crew, who names there crew, what was he 17.

These lame ass niggas followed. Namingyo crew was inviting the FEDS to lock away your whole family. When they bring us down it will simply be the Alton Cartel, because that is the only name the boys will brand me as.

"Yo nigga pass the blunt" Dinero says taking the blunt and laughing.

"This nigga sloppy, he do the same shit every day. That make him a mark for the Alphabet boys and any crew that want to take him out." Dinero said just what I was thinking. I snatched the el from my brother and took a hard pull. "Yet this the nigga they sending for me." I laugh pass the blunt back and start to follow Money as close as I could without him spotting me. This nigga had me laughing, when my phone rang. I looked at Nya's number and laughed she had already came to her senses. "Yo" Dinero says answering the phone when I realize, my wife was calling my brother not me. He shot me a side eye and I shook my head thinking maybe I should have killed my wife years ago.

Lanya

Sacario always tries to hurt, me well fuck him the words I said to him was a long time coming. However I didn't truly mean them it felt good to shake that nigga up.

I did miss my husband, shit he was my husband, and I just didn't know how to tell his ass the entire situation. What was really killing me that Keith was black mailing me, and I felt as if I had no one to turn to. I had kept the fact that Keith could be Deuce's father a secret. Shit I had kept the fact that I had slept with his brother so long I began to forget it until I looked at Deuce standing next to Ali the other day, and since then I have been unable to shake the thought. However I knew the truth Keith was Deuces father. I also knew it was only one other person that knew and maybe willing to help. I fought myself, but I knew that I had to tell someone.

"Yo" Dinero says and I freeze.

"Man what?" I cleared my throat and shook it off.

"O Is Cario with you?" It was a silent pause then he laughed

"Yeah hold on—,"

"No" I yelled "I need to talk to you! Alone. Can you meet me at my house in an hour?"

"For what man?" He asked and I got so upset.

"Because, Dinero I need my big brother! Damn," I cried in his ear ending the call and just falling to the floor.

I knew Dinero and I had not spoken in a while, but he was the only one I knew to go to. He had always been my protector. Shit maybe that was the problem and it was time for me to protect myself.

Dinero

I ended my call with Lanya wanting to be her big brother as I had always been, however I truly didn't want to cross my brother. Fuck so much shit was going on. It was hard for me to think

"Fuck she want?" Killa asked and I really didn't know how to reply.

"Shit she said she need to talk to me about something, but I knowhow—,"

"Naw nigga go head holla at her, ask her why the fuck she playing games."

I laughed knowing my brother was dead ass serious. However I was not about to get in the middle of their shit. I still planned to see what Nya wanted, but he wasn't in the right mind frame to go with me. I had Killa drop me off at home. I needed to check on my wife, plus I needed to see that Nya was good.

~ ~ ~ ~

I walked in my house and it was clear that shit was off. Kym was gone; however her mother was sitting in my son's room watching him sleep. I peaked my head in and went to my room showered and shaved. I tossed on a pair of jogging pants and a v neck T and timberlands. I really didn't know what Nya wanted, but whatever it was I wanted to be ready. I grabbed an extra clip from my safe noticing that 2 bricks of my coke was gone. I got a sour ass face. My girl had been acting nuts then on top of that drugs come up missing shit needed to get back on track and fast. I grabbed my keys and phone and headed out the door. Once Killa and Nya got they shit right maybe me and Kym would get back right.

Chapter 19: A Love like that

Lanya

I didn't expect Dinero to show up, but I won't deny it felt good to be his little sister again. Truth I missed my brother. I missed the whole family. I had been feeling torn and lost. With Keith out of jail, and blackmailing me I really was feeling on edge. Still I couldn't tell him my situation leaving me even more lost. I was so nervous that I had started to drink. I knew it was a bad habit, but it kept my mind off the problems that I faced. The sound of laughter filled my ears I quickly downed the glass of 1800 that sat before me and wiped my mouth with the back of my hand.

"Hey ma" Deuce kissed my right cheek and his best friend Jayson kissed my left one.

"Hey how are my boys" I questioned walking away from the bar towards the kitchen. I love Jayson like my son, because truthfully he was my son. My step son at least crazy thing was that. He nor Sacario new the truth. However I'm no fool I had him DNA tested. Something I still feared doing with Deuce. Once it was confirmed he was Sacario's I began to send Anita Nikiki's mother checks. It was the least I could do after killing Nikiki. Shhh don't tell. But that bitch was trying to make good on having my husband killed; so I sent Saint to body her.

Ihad no problem doing for Jayson my request was for Anita to wait till Sacario was out of jail before I told him and she agreed. Then she came to me telling me that Nikki's fiancé wanted to take care of him. A part of me wanted to say no, but I had already shared Sacario with so many others I agreed still sending Anita money to keep our secret. I never thought that I would see the little boy, leave it to my son to go to school and become friends with his own brother. I couldn't be upset Jayson was a sweet kid that I had started to fall in love with and wished that he was mine. He even called me ma that made me smile.

"Ma where you going" Jayson asked and I smiled looking at he and Deuce standing with their arms crossed over their chest like they could whoop my ass. I walked into the kitchen and they followed. I opened the refrigerator and handed them both a drink.

"Come on ma where you going dressed like that?" Deuce asked referring to the black Gucci dress I had on and matching heels.

"I have a date," I smiled thinking about Jayce. He was no Sacario but he had been a great distraction. Within the last three months that I had been seeing him. He had spent so much time with me. He even ordered that I stop working for my uncles. I was hesitant at first, but he assured me that I would not want for anything and it was for my best interest. I had been a kept woman before and that got me alone and, broke. However I wanted this to be different. So I made sure to keep a side hustle going while maintaining the act of being Jayce's woman.

"A date?" Both boys said in unison following me out the kitchen as the doorbell chimed.

"Ma stop playing, what pops say?" Deuce asked as I opened the door and both boys stood to see who I was going out with.

"Hey beautiful," Jayce says he's holding what looks like hundreds of red and pink roses. He leans in kissing my cheek then placing the roses in my hand.

"Money," Deuce questions and I turn to look at my son.

"Pops?" Jayson says and I damn near lose it shifting my body to face Jayson.

"Ma please tell me you not going out with Money?" Deuce said and I looked over to Jayce

"Deuce is your son?' Jayce asked sucking his teeth.

"Yes he's my son, how do you know— I paused looking at all three of their faces it was as if they all knew something I didn't. Jayce kissed my cheek and took the flowers handing them to the boys.

"Put these in some damn water" Jayce ordered. Grabbing my arm and rushing me out the house like he was pissed.

"Jayce, what's going on?" I asked trying not to panic. However he was upset and didn't seem as he felt like answering questions. He opened my car door and slammed just as I sat down. He had never been this upset the whole three months we had been seeing each other. He rushed to his side of the car and took off. We were on the freeway before I could even blink

"Babe what's wrong?" I asked stroking his arm he looked at me and pulled up at his house. We had only been here once, and it was not the plan to come here. He jumped out and walked around to my door still not speaking a word. I could see the vanes throbbing in his neck and I was hesitant about getting out of the car.

"Man come on," he roared at me and I crossed my legs refusing to move. Jayce seemed on edge as he yanked me out the car, I fell to the ground and Jayce just slammed the door. He grabbed my arm and pulled me to the front door. He unlocked the door and pushed me inside, Jayce was so rough with me. My heart was pounding and I won't lie I felt uncomfortable around him.

"Jayce take me home" I ordered and he slammed and locked the door. I made my way off the ground to the door when he shoved me down again and I didn't even blink before a gun surfaced from his waist band. I mean I knew Jayce was living the street life, but he had never treated me like a common whore. And that's the feeling I was getting at that moment.

Jayce what did I do? I asked not really caring, just wanting to get away from him. I was truly feeling as if he was unstable.

I really didn't know why. We had been having so much fun and he never made sex an issue witch slowly had me falling for him and wanting to make that move with him. Nevertheless the way he was acting tonight all bets were off. In that moment I missed Sacario and knew that Jayce was just a distraction. My phone began to ring and I reached inside my purse looking at Jayce as he held that gun.

"Nero" I said speaking into my phone when the cold feel of steel touched my face.

"Sis where you at Killa say he needs to talk to you and you not at home!"

"O I'm – Jayce snatched the phone and tossed it into the wall.

"So what Nya, you was gone set me up?" he asked pressing the gun in my shoulder. "Go" he ordered and I obeyed. He led me up stairs to his bedroom and I paused. In the last 16 years I had been raped beat kidnapped and raped again. I knew where this was leading and I would not be able yo stand it again. I would kill myself if I had to suffer again. I tried to think of a happy place, as I walked into his bed room. I was sick of being a victim.

"Look Jayce I don't know what you thought that I was gone do; or even what I had done, but I am not that chick. Whatever you brought me here to do, is nothing worse than I have been through." He sucked his teeth and looked my body over his stare was so cold.

"Who would think you would end up with Sacario Killa Alton; do you have no loyalty to family?" He asked stepping into my space.

"Loyalty to who? The one man that has taken care of me? The one man that has loved me, that has been a fuckin man? Unlike yo sick – he didn't allow me to finish before his hand brushed against my face with all his force. I felt my body lift from the ground and my teeth dug in to my tongue right before my body hit the wall. Blood filled my mouth. I couldn't help but wish I would just sit my ass down and listen to my husband. If I make it out of this I will, listen and do as Sacario says. I'm not built for this life and somehow I think that I can take on the world. I thought to myself as a sharp pain shot through my back. I felt him grip my hair tightly and toss me into the wall. Jayce began to rip my clothes off and my heart began to race. I closed my eyes and pictured Sacario. I knew what Jayce was gone to do, and men had taken sex from me so much I really didn't have any feeling down there. In fact I was losing feeling period. They did it to punish me and at this point sex had become meaningless.

He pressed my body against the huge picture window and kissed my body. A chill shot down my spine and I felt my heart go cold.

"Jayce please I love you don't" I mumbled it, but I knew he heard me. His dick rubbed against my ass and I pushed my body back turning to face him. He allowed me to look at him and I leaned in for a kiss.

"Babe why are you so mad?" I asked again not really caring just wanting to get through this night. I wrapped my arms around his neck and continued to kiss him.

"Baby what I do?" I asked and he kissed me sweetly.

"You mine say it Lanya!" He ordered and I pulled back looking in his eyes. God why did every man need to fuckin own me. I closed my eyes and bent in to kiss him he bit my bottom lip as hard as he could his hands palm my breast and his eyes looked into mine. "Say it LaLa." My body shivered he called me a name that no one had called me in a while.

"I'm yours Jayce," I pulled away hitting his shoulder

"Damn Jayce that shit hurt." I bent to pick my 600 dollar dress off the ground. It was destroyed.

"You need to tell me what's wrong with you or I'm leaving" I demanded to know as he looked me over once again. He grabbed my hand and pulled me close.

"You were made for me you know that right" I pulled back looking at my nude body.

"And this is how you treat me?" I sighed walking over to the bed and sitting down.

"Look ma I don't like or trust that nigga Killa" He killed yo pops and he turned you against us."

"Us who the hell is us, and Sacario turned me against no one!"

"That nigga is a shady ass nigga he had my girl killed and --

He paused and walked over to me standing between my legs.

"Baby that nigga no good for you on my word. Jayce said pulling me to my feet. I rolled my eyes and stood up. I need a T shirt and I need your phone to call my kids." Jayce handed me his phone and lied in the bed. "Come lay next to me." He ordered and I sighed looking at the phone placing it on the night table and crawling in the bed beside him. My mind was racing and all I could think is how everyone kept telling me how bad Cario was for me. I knew Jayce wanted to fuck so I gave in and gave him what he wanted, however my mind was not into it.

Money

I woke up with Lanya in my arms and my first thought was of Nikki. I missed her and it was no doubt in my head that Sacario bitch ass had her killed. I hated that nigga for so many reasons, and was mad that I was starting to fall for his wife. I didn't want her to feel like a pawn, but that is what she was about to be come. Lanya and I stayed up all night talking, I even filled her in on the fact that her father use to tell me that he wanted me to protect his baby girl. She lied under me and smiled listing to my every word. I loved that I could be myself with her. She never judged me and she didn't stay mad about how rough I was. A part of me thinks she enjoyed fighting before sex. We had went three rounds, and I could tell that no man made her feel the way I did.

"What time is it?" Lanya asked sitting up

"Morning babe," I walked over to the bed bending to kiss her and she turned her head

"It 7:30 and I can't get a fuckin kiss?" She jumped out the bed and ran into the bathroom.

"Fuck my daughter will be home from camp in twenty minutes, why didn't you wake me?" She yelled now pacing the room. "I need clothes Jayce I have to fuckin go, and look at my fuckin face!" She yelled I looked up noticing her busted lip and the red dash under her eye.

"Damn babe I'm sorry come here let daddy..."

"Jayce can we fuckin go," she say slipping into a pair of my boxers and a t shirt. I grabbed her and looked her over, "Fuck is wrong with you?" She snatched away and picked up her shoes and purse and started out the bed room. This bitch had gone from being my babe to a hoe I wanted to smack. I slipped on a pair of ball shorts and a wife beater and headed out the door.

≈≈≈≈≈≈

The drive felt long and awkward. The more I tried to change Lanya's mood the worse it got. She sat with her hands crossed over her chest and staring out the window.

"Babe what's up?"

"Jayce you were gone rape me, you beat me ruined my clothes and I have to walk in front of my son looking like this where is that ok?

"Lanya bae I said I was..,"

"No the fuck you did not and sorry not gone change the fact that I have a black eye and a busted lip. Whatever Jayce I'm just a hoe to you just like I was my husband." We pulled in to her gate and her guard looked into the car like he wanted to kick my ass as he stared at her face.

"I'm fine Saint I got into a bar fight" She said to him going in her purse pulling out a pair of Gucci sun glasses. I don't know why she didn't put those on earlier. I pulled up and parked the car as I started to get out she grabbed my hand. "You shouldn't come in."

"What?" She cut her eyes at me pulled her keys from her purse and opened her car door.

"I will call you Jayce I just need to..."

"Nah I'll pick you up tonight, I'm not fuckin sleepin alone. I love you." I tell her pulling her over to kiss her and she gave me her cheek.

"I'm sorry baby!" She opens the door and walks onto her porch refusing to look back as she storms inside. I pull off looking at her guard thinking how I wanted to blow his brains out. We gave each other a stern look before I eased back on to the road towards Flint.

Chapter 20

The King of Detroit! Flint Money

After spending so much time with Lanya she opened my eyes to a lot of things I'm sure she had no idea of what she had told me just by telling me that Sacario was staying with his brother the cop. I had no Idea that Ali was a fuckin Fed, but I damn sure was gone make use of it. As I drove to Flint I made a few calls to my inside men. Niggas that I knew could help me take this nigga out. I pulled into the bar and the nigga Smooth was already here. As soon I walked in I could smell his funky ass cheap cigar and I wanted to throw the fuckup.

"Young Blood what's the word?" Smooth asked as I made yet another phone call. I cut my eyes at him and continued my phone call, but like a child he kept talking to me. I sat the phone on the bar pulled my gun and popped the nigga in his knee cap.

"Oh you dumb bitch you don't know who the fuck I am."

"Honestly you a nobody I keep allowing to stick around. I said watching him rock back and forth holding his knee and crying like a bitch. I continued my phone call. I went on to explain what I wanted done and how we would do it when the sound of a gun cocking got my attention. I turned to see Smooth had his huge desert Eagle pointed at me. I pulled my gun back out, but before I knew it I was falling backwards my gun firmly in my hand. I laughed at the way everything was playing out, simply because I should have killed; this nigga years ago and took my rightful place as King of Flint. Under my leadership and his connections I would have been took Sacario nevertheless it would end in my favor. Smooth stood over me his bloody hand wrapped around his gun, he could barely stand. The door to the bar opened and he took his eyes off me for one second I raised my gun and emptied my clip.

"Boss you good" Twan and Desmond asked. They had made it to the bar in record time. Twan stood me to my feet and I held my shoulder and rushed to remove the gun from Smooth's now dead body. I had to save face until I got the connect from Dice so I stood holding Smooth's gun and fired at the door the first shot was off because my arm was stiff and sore but the second one went into Desmond's head. Twan jumped and I smiled handing him the gun. Get somebody to clean this mess up. I searched the bar for my phone calling Dice.

"We took fire" I yelled into the phone, "It don't look good I told Dice before ending the call. Twan gave me a slight smile and I nodded for him to go. He would have to carry my plans out.

Chapter 21

KARMA is A Bitch

Lanya

"...Aha! Hmmm! Hmm

I, I, I, I've been through some things,

Please don't hold that against me,

Can't nobody love you like I'm gonna love you

Can't nobody love you like I'm gonna love you

Even though I, I, I still can feel a sting,

No need to second guess me,

Can't nobody love you like I'm gonna love you

Can't nobody love you like I'm gonna love you..."

JENNIFER HUDSON blasted in my ear; She was telling a man that no one could love him like she did and in that moment it was the song my heart sung.

Why was he doing this to me? I waited seven years to sleep in his arms, seven years to kiss his lips, oh and the longest seven years in life to feel his hard wood inside of my teapot. Didn't he know that I needed him? Did he care? I wondered if I still owned a place in Sacario's heart. I guess that's what had me feeling like a stalker. Tears trailed my cheeks, as I sat in my car across the street; from Ali's house. I took a deep breath, and fired up a blunt that I had found in my sons room and slumped down in my car seat. My eyes fixed on the three cars parked in the yard. Only two really had me frustrated one being the cocaine white Yukon and the second the Barbie pink S class. Taking a pull from the blunt I sing along with J Hud and tried my best not to lose my mind. He had that bitch living in Ali's house while I stayed up night with, knots in my stomach on my knees praying that he came home to me. It was clear to me that 16 years met nothing to this nigga. I took another pull and hit the steering wheel, with both hands. I don't know if it was the buzz from the Kush, or the pure anger I was feeling that Sacario just didn't love me anymore, but this was some bull shit and I was sick of taking and dealing with everyone's bullshit. I took one last pull, and opened my car door, tossing the blunt to the ground. I don't know what I was gone to say or how I was gone to do it, but I was gone to be heard. I slammed my car door and charged to the front door. My heart must have been racing because I could hear my pulse in my ears, and my brow was now completely covered in sweat. I ran on Ali's porch and began to bang and scream

Sacario's name. "Cario I know you are in here nigga open the fuckin door." I yelled pounding the solid oak door with both fist. Ali's neighbors were now standing on their porches, as I could give a fuck.

Finally Ali opened the door, and before he could say a word I pushed the door as hard as I could into him running in his house, and up the stairs. I walked into the first bed room it was empty so I rushed into the second one Sacario was sitting on the bed like he was waiting for me. He was topless with a pair of ball shorts and timberlands on his feet. As mad as I was I couldn't deny that he was by far the sexiest man that God had ever created. "What the fuck is wrong with you?" He asked nonchalantly. I crossed my arms over my chest trying to catch my breath I rolled my eyes was this nigga serious. I thought to myself as I looked around the bedroom. "Where is she at?" I asked tears already forming in my eyes.

"Man get the fuck on with that shit Nya! Nobody here!" He says and his eyes drift to the bathroom door. "That's where that bitch at Cario, really you can't even be honest with me." I ran to the bathroom door kicking it. "Fuck is you doing?" Sacario yelled grabbing my arms. I looked back at him elbowing him in his chest. Kicking the door one last time and watching it fly open. I pulled

195

myself from his grip and walked in the bathroom looking at that bitch Olivia hiding like the dirty piece of side trash she was. I charged towards her and Sacario grabbed me, but I already held a handful of her hair in my hand. As he pulled me back I pulled her with me. My fist, were still pounding into her head. I could feel saliva fall from my mouth; as it hung open and I cried and screamed with every punch. "Nya stop it," I hear Sacario yell still holding my body with one hand and trying to get my hands from her hair.

Ali lifted me from Sacario's arms and dragged me into another bedroom and slammed the door. I held my fist tightly closed still holding a handful of the bitch Olivia's hair in my hand. I went from hyperventilating to just crying as Ali held me close and tight. "What is she doing here? What did I do Lee? What did I do?" I questioned repeatedly. Ali guided me to the bed he sat down and pulled me between his legs. "Nya calm down." He said rubbing my back as I held his neck tightly. "Lee what did I do because I love my husband!"

"Nya you didn't do shit," he told me sitting me on his lap and running his hands through my hair. He then strokes my face and I rested my head on his shoulder. "Fuck is this shit Bro?" Sacario said busting into the room ripping me out of Ali's arm. Ali sprung to his feet and stepped into Sacario's space. "We got a problem?" Sacario questioned Ali.

"Naw nigga you got this!" Ali says bumping shoulders with Sacario as he walked out of the room. "You a real piece of work Killa," I say spitting his street name. He hated for me to do it, but I love to piss him off. "Man Lanya watch ya fuckin words!"

"Yeah Killa cuz words hurt more than walking in on the only man I have ever loved and some half dressed bitch, that you sent to do yo dirty work. You a dick I hate that I love yo bitch ass—," I couldn't finish the statement before Sacario tossed me into the closet wall, his hand around my neck. His eyes looked into mine I felt as if he was looking into my soul. I felt almost as if he had ripped my heart from my body with those actions alone.

"Nya no man loves you more than I do, but who the fuck gone kiss somebody ass for 20 years to be with them. You want me; then you don't give a fuck, you need to keep it fuckin real. You can't get mad every time you see a bitch on my dick then spit I'm not yo husband." He lowered me, and I grabbed my neck.

"You right..."

I cleared my throat and made it to my feet. "We over, just know that for here on out, I don't belong to you. Not my kisses not my pussy, and damn sure not my heart. I pushed pass Sacario, when he grabbed my arm and pulled me into his space. I was looking back into those eyes that drove me insane.

"Baby can we go now?" The voice from behind me asked, and realize that no matter how much I love this man we will never be.

≈ ≈ ≈ ≈ ≈ ≈

I never drove so fast in my life. Tears flooded my eyes and the image of her and him in my head I couldn't clearly understand how any man can walk away from a woman he claimed to love, but after 16 years I was completely at a lost. The same question flashed in my head, and that only made me cry harder.

I could barely see as I raced down I 75 I didn't even live this way, and truth I had no Idea where I was going, but I just knew I wanted to forget that Sacario Lamar Alton ever existed.

Crazy because Ali was all that I could think of. The way he held me and truly cared that I was hurt. The way I felt when I was in his arms. God I know that was so wrong of me, however I couldn't control who filled my head; as I pulled up in front of Jayce's house. I was no fool; I could never be with Lee. That was just too much; loving my husband's brother that was crazy. I told myself as I stepped out of my car and ran to the front door. I didn't care that I was a mess, my body and heart was numb, and I felt as if I was the walking dead. I paused as I got to the door and thought about the conversation that I had, had with Dinero and I had weeks before. I knew that being with Jayce was a bad Idea, but I had to do something. I needed to feel GOD I just wanted to know I was alive. I rushed to the door and pressed the doorbell repeatedly. My hands shook butterflies filled my stomach as I prayed silently that Jayce would hurry to the door. The sound of my phone ringing only made me even more impatient. I glanced down to see Ali's name and my heart began to ache. The door flew open and I came face to face with Jayson.

"Hey ma you ok?" He says to me now guilt consumed me, I was living a lie my life was a mess I was here blaming, Sacario for not loving me, when I had hired Saint to kill the mother of his child. Paid the only other person that knew Jayson's true identity so that I could keep my happy family and here Karma was kicking my ass. Ten years I had lived and hid a lie and now it was looking me in my face I almost felt as if I would lose it in that moment. "Hey baby" Jayce says walking down the stairs. Jayson bends to kiss my face as he walks out the door and I rush to Jayce.

In my mind I knew I was about to cross every line that I knew I shouldn't, but what did I care. I had already sold my soul to be happy and look how unhappy it had made me. I rested my head on Jacye's chest and he receives me without a problem. I let my body go and I fall motionless in his arms. "Lanya, babe you alright?" Jayce said lifting me to his arms. I could hear Sacario's voice in my head telling me to think before I did what I planned on doing. I didn't care I placed my lips on Jayce's pillow soft lips and ran my fingers up the back of his head resting my hand on the nape of his neck, as he carried me into his bed room. "Love me Jayce" I beg him to do for me what I couldn't do for myself thirty two years old and I still hadn't learned how to love myself. He laid me on his king size bed and I began to rip at his clothes. I sat up on my knees and lifted his shirt over his head.my hands roamed his chest, and everything about Jayce was sexy. His dark brown skin, was the color of cognac, his well sculpted body. He didn't have a six pack or anything; however his arms and chest were of perfection. He came closer and I allowed myself to relax. My lips explored Jayce's body his hands intertwined in my hair. My vagina was screaming for his dick, I spread my legs slipping my hand into my pants. Closing my eyes I rubbed my clit finally giving Jayce a chance to trace my body with his pillow soft lips. I unfastened my pants, and Jayce was quick to assist. He knocked me on my back and yanked my pants off. He bent kissing my stomach and ripped my panties off. His tongue moved fast going from my stomach to right inside my cream. I purred like a kitten lifted my legs and pushed his head in deeper. He sucked and slurped like I needed him to do. "Oh yes daddy I love you," I yelled. Jayce lifted his head and smiled climbing on top of me and kissing my lips. It was that second that I realized he was not Sacario. He was the only man that I wanted inside of me. I knew it was too late when I felt the hardest pipe I had felt in a long time split me open I dug in to Jayce and screamed God, but I cried Cari. I gave Jayce my body in that moment, but my husband had my heart and soul. "Yes Baby I love you" Jayce said slowing his pumps. He held my body tighter as he grinded but I could see in his eyes he was ready to unload. "Baby pull out kay" I whispered in his ear and he found strength going harder. I tried to pull away, but Jayce grabbed my hair and twisted his hand in it he forced me over on my stomach my head twisted to look at him as he pumped a few more times and unloaded in me. He licked his lips and smiled. "My name is Money see if that nigga Killa want yo ass when my baby grow in you." Jayce said letting me know he heard the cries I said for Cari. Money stood to his feet and walked in the bathroom leaving me in my thoughts.

Three weeks had passed and I hadn't spoken with either Jayce or Sacario. In fact neither had even called me three weeks. I was starting to feel dumb as hell. I looked down as my cellphone began to vibrate and it was Dinero. The one person that had been calling constantly and ironically enough I had been avoiding his calls. I picked up the phone not really wanting to even say hello. "Yo baby sis I'm on my way over we need to talk." Nero says and I roll my eyes. "About what Nero"

"You need to watch ya tone, but that nigga Keith you been fucking, him?" He asked with concern in his voice. "Dinero I told you he was back, because I wanted you to be there for me, I don't need you judging me." I snapped Dinero was about to open a door I wasn't ready to open. I could hear Nero talk, but now my mind was back on Keith and our last meeting. He had hit me up for a quarter of a million dollars, and forced me to have sex with him one last time. It hurt so bad that I bled, he wouldn't allow me to clean myself, Keith just rushed me to get the cash. I was still necked and bloody when Sacario and Ali walked in. I was also sure that I smelt like open ass, because that was the hole Keith preferred now days.

"Nya you hear me" Nero ask and I shook off the thought

"What O, what did you say?"

"Nya nigga is a fiend I seen him shooting up, at one of the houses, and he was sharing needles with a nigga I know he got that shit!

"What shit Nero" Oh my God my heart was racing and tears were ready to fall. I couldn't breathe and Dinero hadn't even said the fuckin letters yet.

"Man NYA he got HIV, sure oh boy got it too, so tell me if you, know. I dropped the phone to the ground I couldn't speak or think my mouth was now dry and I could taste Keith's lips on mine.

That was the perfect punishment for the bastard however what did I do to deserve it. I couldn't breathe as I fell to the floor. I pulled myself together thinking of Deuce and Lyssa my babies; I needed to make sure they would be good. I guess Sacario should thank the Gods above he was with Olivia, I couldn't win for always losing I went from being raped, beat , lied to , and mistreated for it to end with me dying of Aids. Oh whatever I did in my past life, I was paying for now.

I picked up my phone and ran my fingers over the screen. All I could think about was Cario. He had always told me that I never tell him when I needed him, but now I had no choice but to tell him. Fuck I thought Jayce. Hell if I don't die from Aid's that thug nigga was gone kill me for, infecting and double crossing him in the same breath. I held down the number 2 watching as Sacario's face popped on the screen. I didn't know what I was gone say, but I just knew I needed him to come.

Sacario

I had been watching Money for almost 6 months, he was becoming reckless. But killing off his so called business partners was one of the dumbest. However fucking my wife was his suicide note signed sealed and delivered. "Morning baby," Olivia says wrapping her arms around me as she sat on my lap. I really tried to get over Nya and make it work with Olivia I had moved into a condo close to Nya's house so I could see my kids more, and no matter how hard I tried to shake Olivia she hung on to me like a wet rag. "Move" I told her standing and answering my ringing phone.

"What?" The caller just breathed into the phone and I knew it was Nya.

"What man?" We hadn't spoken in damn near a month. She called herself being mad at me, for being with Olivia. Well I was beyond pissed at my wife for not being my fucking wife. When I got home, she was supposed to fall back in my arms and say I do one last time. I fuckin loved my wife; I get out too find out she fuckin every dick moving.

"I need help, I'm in over my head!" Lanya cries and I scratch my head as I look at Olivia walking towards me.

"Man Nya I don't understand what the fuck it is you want me to do?" I hold my hand out pushing Olivia away she crossed her hands over her chest, poking her lip out like I give a damn that she upset.

"Cari I need you, I thought I could—

"Look Nya you wanted freedom so I'm giving it to you."

"I always needed you Cari; I just needed you not to cheat. I needed you to come home Sacario; You know what fuck it forget I fuckin…"

"Babe"

"No Fuck it Killa we over you divorced me and I been paying ever since"

"Nya I told you why I did..."

"You know what Sacario save it! Go fuck yo bitch! Be with your hoes I don't care, just make sure that's what ..." She ended the call I could hear the pain in her voice, but I couldn't worry about that I needed my mind to be clear so I could do what I needed to do. Olivia wrapped her arms around my waist and began to kiss my neck. I pushed back and was really starting to get pissed. I walked in the bathroom and showered, just as Olivia climbed in I hopped out.

I know that we had, been fuckin but she knew I had a wife and this was just business. I need Olivia to work her magic with customs, and a few other overseas connect she had to get the land I was trying buy. She started off understanding that, but once I gave Lanya a divorce, somehow she thought that meant me and her were a couple.

"Sacario!"

"What Olivia?"

"That's how you treat me after all we have been through one call from that busted fat bitch and you gone!" I couldn't help but laugh.

"You know I divorced my wife , because you told me they would come after her, You told me that because she had my last name they were opening cases, so I know you know that we never truly had shit, because I love my wife.

"Oh now you love the bitch, you didn't love her when I was sucking yo dick last night"

"Yeah I did I loved her every time you sucked my dick or I busted on yo face, she my wife your business pussy." I walked over to my dresser and grabbed a blunt that I had rolled earlier and my lighter and lit it. Olivia looked at me speechless and in tears and I shook my head as I took a pulled and held it out for her to take. She smacked my hand and I smiled taking another pull and putting it out with my two fingers I sat the blunt down and walked in the closet and started to dress.

≈≈≈≈≈≈

I pulled up to my wife house to see my son sitting on the front steps talking on his phone.

"What up son?" He nodded and I sat beside him.

"You been good?"

"Yeah pops," he shot me a look and I smiled

"Nigga—," I had to stop myself from cutting into him. I hopped up and walked to the door, "come holla at ya old man when you done." I tell him as I proceeded into the house.

"Nya Babe where you at?" I shouted running up stairs I opened the bed room door and let my eyes wonder when I saw my wife's body lying still on the floor a bottle of pills beside her.

I looked at my wife and my heart stopped my feet glued to the floor. I couldn't move. No matter what my mind told me to do; my body wouldn't allow it. Flashes of my parents ran through my head and in that second I hated Nya. I told her my past and that was the one thing I thought was weak in a nigga, to see her there I didn't know how to feel.

"Ma" I hear my son say from behind me and I turn to grab him.

"Man move, the fuck" Deuce says and I hold him tighter not wanting him to see what I had to.

"Fuck yo bitch ass do to her?" He says and just as I go to slam him my brother walks into the room.

"Fuck going on Dinero says and I freeze as he pushes past Deuce and I and lifts Nya in his arms. "Nigga call 911 she still breathing" Nero yells and I look at Deuce as he pushes away from me and dials 911.

Dinero

I looked at my brother and knew what he was thinking. I also knew what Nya had been going through. I thought back to the day she called me over. Lanya was in a panic she really didn't know how to deal with everything that what was going on

She told me about her step farther and asked me to just be her big brother not step in, but me being her big brother how could I not step in. I told her I wouldn't lay hands on boy if she did what I needed her to do. She gave me those sad eyes however agreed to the plan. I knew that she had been working with her uncles, and by now I was sure they wanted to take us out. I needed Nya to get as close as possible and find out what they were planning, and who they had competing with us. I knew it was Money and he was no threat to us, nevertheless I just wanted to make sure she was still team Alton. I couldn't afford for anyone to be disloyal at this point.

"O they here" Sacario said as a man puts oxygen to Lanya's mouth and I assist him to lie her on the gurney. "Deuce where yo sister" I ask and he walks out the room like he didn't hear me. Deuce wasn't my son, but he had never disrespected me. He walked back in my niece on his shoulder sleep; I took her out his hands and started out the bedroom. My brother was no longer insight and Deuce was already on the phone.

≈ ≈ ≈ ≈ ≈ ≈

We all stood front and center in the hospital waiting room. Kym rocked Alyssa while Killa paced the hospital floor. I looked over to my nephew who was texting his ass off. "DA fuck happened Ali walked in to the lobby overconfident stride and condescending ass smile. He had that egotistical look in his face that he always had when he walked in the room. Don't get me wrong I loved both my brothers, but the way Ali acted as if he was God's gift always made me a little sour. Deuce jumped out of his seat and ran to Lee they hugged and began to huddle. I always questioned why they had such a close relationship, but I guess he remained close to them when Nya shut me out. Twenty minutes later Ali made his way to the chair beside me. "What he say to her?" Ali whispered and I sucked my teeth, "She was already like that when he found her" Ali nodded and looked back at Deuce

"Well D seems to think they were fighting what up with that?"

"Nigga all I know is he walked in the room and she was laying there note was on the bed, but Killa tossed it before the EMT got to the house." Ali's phone began to buzz he looked at it and put it to his ear. I listened to the one sided phone call for a second, but Killa was stressing me pacing like he was on the verge of losing it. I stood and walked over to him and grabbed him walking him to a chair. "Nigga you being pissed off not gone help yo wife." "Fuck said it would?" I faced my brother knowing he was thinking unclearly.

"Nigga I'm not one of yo hoe's."

"Fuck said you were? Nigga get out my face with that shit!"

"Yo I'm gone let shit slide because where we at, but you need to watch yo tone" I tell Sacario taking the seat. He jumps up and kick the chair, "man lets go fuck this selfish bitch." He walked over to Kym picking up Aylssa who was sleeping in her arms.

"She fine Cario," Kym said trying not to wake her. Lee jumped up grabbing Killa trying to calm him but he was in no way hearing anyone. "Man fuck that hoe I'm out!" Sacario started towards the door, but my nephew was in his father's face. His shoulders were up right and in no way was he backing down. "You a bitch ass nigga!" Deuce said stepping to Killa they were squared off in the middle of the hospital like niggas on the street. "Nigga who the fuck you talkin to?"

"Yo bitch ass, how the fuck you gone treat her like she nothing, then get mad she did what the fuck she did? You a Bitch!" Sacario stepped in Deuce face and I quickly grabbed Sacario, while Ali pulled Deuce away. They both were heated and truly not willing to back down. I pulled Sacario out of the hospital. I walked my brother over to my truck we both hopped in and I fired up a blunt. "Man that nigga got the right name?" I tell Sacario referring to Deuce. "Fuck you mean my nigga?"

"That nigga a hot head just like his daddy," I took a hit from the blunt and passed the blunt to my brother. He took two pulls before the tears started to fall. "Nigga why would she do this? Why I didn't just tell her I was coming? Fuck!" He yelled handing me the blunt. I felt guilty knowing that the reason Nya did it was my fault.

"O she my wife, I can't lose her, I love her I just needed her to see—Fuck!" He yelled watching as Deuce and Lee walked out the hospital. Killa jumped out the truck and walked over to Deuce. I was sure it would be round two. Sacario stepped in Deuce face and they both were squared off again.

"Sacario I'm your fuckin father! You may be pissed as fuck, but never do you show that shit to any man." He told his son pulling him in his arms hugging him. Deuce hugged his father just as tight.

"Pops she been crying for so long, what if she don't fight man? What if she die!?"

"Yo mother is strong as fuck, she not gone die!" He went into his pocket handing his son a wad of cash. "Yo get yo sister, take her home, feed her I will be there tonight—,"

"Dad—,"

"D, I will be there, I know I fucked up but no more I'm coming home. You don't have to take care of your mom anymore that's my job." Sacario assured Deuce walking back to my truck and hopping in. Lee got in the backseat and we sat in silence.

"Yo why she do it?" Ali asked and I knew I had to come clean with my brothers. I took a deep breath and looked at Killa, knowing that he was gone freak out.

"It's my fault!" All eyes were on me! I really didn't want to say any more, but Killa and Lee both gave me their undivided attention.

"What you mean yo fault? Fuck you do?" Killa asked and I knew this would be the hardest thing I had to do.

"Bout two months ago Nya came to me telling me that her uncle's wanted her to set me up. She told me that she knew we hadn't talked in a while, but we were the only family she truly had. She also told me that her stepfather was back in her life." Neither man made a sound; it was then I knew they knew nothing about Lanya's past.

"You don't know do you?" I asked my brother and Ali smirked.

"Know what nigga get to the fuckin point." Killa said and I dropped my head, feeling like all I had done was a mistake. "Nya's old dude the doctor?" I looked at Lee and he nodded.

"The nigga that was at the house the other day I knew I had saw his bitch as before." Lee said and now I was lost.

"Nigga go head!" Killa ordered.

"Anyway when she was a kid he raped her! He raped her alot to the point that she don't know if you, or him is Deuce's dad."

"Nigga that's my son!" My brother cut me off pulling his gun from his waist band.

"Anyway nigga he went to jail, and now he out and blackmailing her. I told her that I wouldn't do shit, to him; inturn I needed her to set up her uncles for me, but I felt like she was hiding something. I mean Nya like my little sister, fuck she is my sister I knew something was wrong, so I lied and told her ol' boy was a fiend and had that shit—,"

"What shit?" Lee asked and Killa and I both gave him the look. "Nigga go head," Killa said cocking his gun but never taking his eyes off me.

"I was trying to see if he was still raping her! I was trying to see if ...."

"So you telling me my wife been living with this shit for sixteen years and you knew?" Killa asked putting his gun in my face.

"Nigga don't pull that shit if you not gone use it!" I told him smacking it out my face. Ali's phone began to ring, however Sacario and I couldn't take our eyes off each other.

"Yo that's the hospital, Nya woke." Lee says and Killa look at his phone.

"We not done!" Killa says to me stepping out the car and walking inside. I can't help but to blame myself.

Chapter 22:

Same Script Different Cast

Lanya

I woke up in the psych ward my head was pounding and my hands were restrained. I didn't know what hurt worse my head, or the fact that no one in my family was in sight. So much was still running through my mind mainly, what Nero had told me about Keith. I just wished that Cario was here to hold me. Wait how did I get here? Oh God thoughts of Deuce finding me like this and that letter I left what was I thinking?. I deserve to be here I thought closing my eyes as tight as possible trying to prevent the tears from making their way out of my eyes. "What the fuck were you thinking?" I hear someone say. I feel his hand run through my hair and pray that it's Cario. My eyes fly open to see Money by side. I was totally beyond shocked. "What are you doing here?" I asked and he smiled making my heart skip a beat. "Shit I'm asking you the same thing, you my girl and I find out you taking bottles of pills and shit." He bent kissing my face and continued running his hands through my hair. I tried to move my hands, but I was still tied down. "Babe calm, yo little self, down. You know they gone keep yo crazy ass in here a week for that dumb shit you pulled!" Jayce says sitting my bed up and pulling the chair in the room beside my bed and sitting down.

"Where are the kids?" I asked looking around.

"Their fine Jayson said he's at your house and they'er eating playing video games."

"Oh God did Sacario see me like this?" Jayce rolled his eyes at me and ran his hand over my stomach, "You pregnant you know that right?" My eyes got as big as quarters. "What the fuck you mean?" I asked him tears really started to pour down my cheek. I'm thirty two years old how I couldnt do this again. Knocked up and not know the father, Lord I have to be the biggest whore in the world, and oh God what if I have HIV. My body started to shake and before I knew it I was covered in my own vomit. Jayce jumped back and looked at me, as my body heaved back and forth and I began to choke on the tones of liquid pouring out of me.

"Can I get a doctor in here?" another voice yells and I feel my face being turned to the side.

"Breathe Nya" I know that it's Sacario, from the smell of 212 that feels the room over the vomit. He rubs my back as I feel more hands pulling at me and undressing me. I'm ripped out of the bed and onto another. Everything moves so fast I start to get even dizzier I fight to keep my eyes open, but a mask covers my face before the room gets black.

Sacario

When I walked into that room and saw Nya on the floor a part of me was so mad at her. The other part begged God to spare here and take me. I couldn't understand why she would hurt me so bad, but picking up and reading that letter showed me how much she loved me. The words written were plan and simple, "I can't live if heis not here" What had I done to my wife, it started off me want to protect her now I was sitting here trying to blame every one for my mistakes.

I can't blame my brother, for not telling me Nya is my wife, I should have known. Better yet she should have fuckin told me.

I know that I have been doing other shit, but why Nya felt like she couldn't talk to me is crazy. This is why we have been so distant, but it's all gone change starting today. The hospital saying she was woke restores my faith and gives me a second chance with my girl.

She said I was the only man she loved, truth she was the one who showed me how to love and no other woman could hold a spot in my heart, because my whole heart belong to my wife. Period! I made a quick stop at the gift shop grabbing up flowers bears candy and any other thing I could find to make my bae smile. My plan was to hurry get her out this spot and take her on a weekend vacation just the two of us. I knew her and Kym weren't talking, but she was gone have to get over that shit and let the kids stay with my brother so I can give her the TLC she needed. As I walked in the room I could barely see, for all the shit I was carrying all I know is that I heard what sound like convulsions. I dropped all the shit and rushed to her side turning her over on her side I pulled her wrist out of those hospital restraints and rubbed her back, assuring her I was there. I tried to calm her best I could as she spilled her insides out. Nonetheless I was beyond calm looking over at Money and wonder, why he was in her room, how he knew she was here, and what he had done to my wife. I yelled for the doctor and when they rushed in and took over I made my move walking up on money, it was no need to pull my gun, this was that nigga I was gone kill with my fuckin hands. This was not the time; nor place. He stood his grounds pretending he feared nothing. I sucked my teeth and made sure he knew that I was ready to end him "Bitch nigga you not bout that life," He says to me and I swing. I didn't intend to go in on this nigga, and he gave as good as he got, but this was not gone be a fight he would win as we wrestled on the floor like school age kids. I could feel him go in on me and I was not gone fall back I felt hands surrounding me and pulling me back, but I didn't fall back till I felt the blood splatter hit my face. I looked down at my chest and felt no pain. In fact I saw no blood other than what was now on my hand. I looked to Money and the niggas mouth was wide open, as he made his way out the door. I shifted my body as I felt a hand touch my shoulder. I lost my breath as I saw my son holding his chest and falling to his knees.

Ali

Lust is an ugly thing, however I don't think what I feel for Nya is lust. I have been in love with her since the day she walked into the bar. I knew I had saw her somewhere before, but nevertheless she was the type of woman I could see myself with. At first she would not give me the time of day, but one night, she looked like she had been through hell and back and I just gave her a shoulder to lean on, I never thought that in that one night we would have mind, blowing sex. I had never been with a woman so passionate so loving in my life, I wanted to keep her in my bed, forever but it was in my bed that I realized all though she had given me her body, her heart was with my brother. As she slept she called out his name. I didn't know they knew each other, and then it hit me she was the girl he picked up from the gas station. That was when I knew I had to fall back. I told her that Sacario would never know,our secret, but it was killing me. Sixteen years later and I was still unable to be with any one always comparing every woman to the one night I spent with Nya. So when Deuce called me telling me that she had taken pills, I walked out the office no thought about it.

Lanya would always be the most important woman to me. Hell not making a move on her when my brother was locked down killed me. That was partly the reason why I kept my distance. The day he was arrested I crossed the line, and I won't deny I would do it again.

Man my eyes must have been playing tricks on me, as I walked towards Nya room I see a slew of people running in, I got closer and I saw two armed guards holding their hands out to stop me I went in my back pocket and pulled my credentials. Walking into the room to see my brother being questioned by two uniform cops.

One had guided him to his knees and placed his hands behind his back as I stepped in.

"What the fuck happened?" I asked my brother. The uniform looked me up and down and smiled. I cleared my throat reached in my pocket pulled my badge, flashing those three letters I dared any nigga not fear. FBI. Again I said what the fuck happened. Both men were speechless as I stood my brother to his feet dug in my pocket pulled my universal hand cuff key and unlocked his cuffs.

"Somebody shot my fuckin son!" Sacario said looking at me.

"Deuce? I questioned knowing that Sacario had two son's that was a secret that he I and Dinero shared. He cut his eyes at me yeah nigga who the fuck else." He rubbed his wrist, and just looked at me with that look he got when he was ready to kill.

Chapter 23:

Definition of love is?

Money

When I met Nikki I was fresh out of jail and not really looking for a relationship, but Nikki was easy to fall for. She told me she just wanted to start over, I definitely could understand that. Nikki had made a mistake and slept with her boss and had his child. This made her desperate for a change. Jayson was two years old, so very impressionable. I had no clue that the father of her child was Sacario, and I couldn't bare to tell Nikki that Sacario and I had history. I didn't know how she would feel if she knew that nigga Killa was one of my closest friends till he got greedy and the nigga Silk ordered me to set him up. It would have worked in my favor if Dinero didn't kill Silk and I was sure that Sacario had figured out it was me, that had shot him years ago. I had no choice, but to shot him and make it look like a robbery. Yeah Sacario was like my brother, but in the game, you really can't trust anyone. So it was a matter of time before he would kill me so I did what I had to do. I never thought that the nigga would live and, take of the game as I rotted away in jail for having a few bags of weed on me.

As if that wasn't enough of a reason for him to want me dead I start fucking his wife and shoot his son fuck my life

Lanya

I woke up my mind fuzzy, my chest was still on fire and my head was pounding. I searched the room for a sign of life besides myself, but no one was in sight. Maybe all that I had seen was a reaction from the pills I had ingested. I thought closing my eyes feeling alone, and wondering what my next step would be. If it all were a dream why was Money the first one I saw? Maybe he was the man that I needed to help me through all of this pain.

"Hey sexy" I turned my head quickly to see who had entered the room.

"Hi Sacario" He held flowers and was dressed in jeans and timberlands. My heart began to race those were the clothes that he kept in his car for emergencies. Sometimes I feared I know my husband to well. "What is it Cario? I questioned preparing myself for the worst. "Damn babe why something gotta be wrong I just wanted to see my favorite girl I missed you?" He bent to kiss me and I turned my head. I really wanted to kiss him, but I thought about the three letters Dinero had said to me.

Adding insult to injury he had been with the bitch Olivia for months, when I saw him I thought of her face.

"Damn ma it's like that you can't kiss yo husband?"

"Yeah let me know when the nigga get here and I will!" I shot back at him with a bull shit ass comment. "Man whatever Nya I need to talk to you ma!" His voice became a little strained and I knew the shoe was about to drop. He pulled the chair and sat down holding his empty hand out for mine. My heart was really racing, oh God it was confirmed I had the shit I could see the sorrow in his eyes. "Sacario you driving me nuts Say it!" He sighed and kissed my hand. "Baby just know that he fine and staying with Lee" I pulled my hand away and sprung up. I looked at Sacario with wide eyes.

"Who's fine Sacario?"

"You don't remember?"

"Clearly I don't damn stop talking in circles what happened?"

"Deuce got shot babe, but he fine. It was a flesh woun...,"

I held my hand up to catch my breath. "You say that shit like he a grown ass man that's my son Sacario—

." He jumped up tossing the flowers on me as the chair he was sitting in hit the floor, "Understand he is our fuckin son Nya so trust I fuckin know, don't think I take shit lightly." I laid back on the bed letting a tear fall. I knew he was right, but I was so use to Sacario being locked up that I had taken the us out of everything.

"Can I see him where is he?" I went to sit on the side of my bed and Sacario pushed me back. "There is more Nya."

"What is more important than my son?" I asked knowing he was talking about my own health. My heart was racing, but I wanted to put me on the back burner and be there for my baby.

Sacario turned his back on me like he was upset with me, I really didn't want to cry, but I could feel it. He walked over to the lockers and pulled out a bag. He then began to unpack the bag pulling clothes and shoes from it.

"You love me Lanya?"

"Fuck that got to do with anything Cari?

"Not a damn thing you right let Money ass come get you!" He was heated, but so was I. I watched as he dug into his pocket pulling out three rings my engagement ring and wedding band and his wedding band. He slammed them on the hospital table and bent down looking in my eyes. "You allowed another man to put a child in yo body, you can't be serious, yet you crying for my love. Our marriage was a fuckin joke so keep the rings, because I'm done, just like that bastards seed I made them rip out yo dumb ass. Know this Lanya you may not be my wife, but you belong to me and you will never carry another niggas shit in you!"

His eyes were full of pain and his mouth full of venom as he ripped me a new ass. I placed my hand over my belly and sighed. Sacario looked at me one last time and started towards the door. I opened my mouth, but the words couldn't, or wouldn't come out.

"Sacario I cried out moments later, but I was sure he was gone. I was feeling more than lost as I stood to my feet and all most passed out as the worse pain imaginable brought me to my knees. It was then I remembered that Jayce had told me I was carrying his child. God my life could get no worse. I thought out loud; quickly covering my mouth knowing that the statement alone would bring on more than I was ready to deal with.

Pushing through the pain I dressed in the clothes that Sacario had just laid out slipping my wedding band only on and the other two rings in my pocket. The nurse walked in the room and instantly began to frown. Mrs. Alton someone has to sign you out. She says guiding me back to the bed.

"Says who?"

"Doctors' orders you have been through a lot in the last seven days—," I held my hand cutting her off.

"Seven days?"

"See Mrs. Alton this is why you need someone to stay with you, I think your husband just left I will call him back. You are a lucky woman, a man sitting by your bedside day and night for a week, that's love." She said and I sighed again

"I'm not married," looking at my wedding band.

"Well some handsome man really loves you, he said he was your husband."

"We're divorced, but that's beside the point I need to see my chart."

"What is it that you would like to know Mrs. Alton?"

"MY NAME IS LANYA MARKS! Damn, and I want to know what procedures I have had." The slender woman walked out of the room, returning ten minutes later with two arm guards. I looked the men over regretting that I said nothing could get worse.

"Basically Mrs. Alton I was told that you attempted to take your own life. Is that true?"

"Not at all?" I lied they were not gone to get me to say that shit out loud I had saw a many movies that ended bad because of some one agreeing with hospital workers. I plopped down on the hospital bed and grabbed the phone that sat beside it. I really didn't know who to call, but my husband was out of the question. I didn't have any family other than his, and again I felt alone. I held the phone and looked at the numbers taking a deep breath and I dialed the one person I thought might come get me.

Sacario

I really don't think that Nya understood how much she meant to me. I mean I fucked up so what we all have the shit that we would take back, but the fact that she let another nigga buss inside her. It killed me to find out she was pregnant. It hurt even worse when they told me that it was killing my wife and my choice rather she carry to term or abort it. Despite the fact that the child wasn't mine, I still didn't want it dead. The words I said to her were in anger. I got in my brothers car taking the blunt from his hand as he lied back, like he had not a care in the world. He started the car and pulled off as I took a pull of the kush filled blunt, and drifted.

"How's the wife doing?" Dinero asked looking a little distant himself.

"She good, what's up with you? why does it look like you not sleeping?"

Dinero took the blunt and pulled up to the bar. His phone had been ringing since he picked me up. "Yo," he said looking over to me he smiled.

"Hey baby sis how you feeling?" I held my hand out for the phone and he held his hand up giving me a finger. He nodded his head a couple times and laughed.

"Baby sis yo man right here, he will be pissed." I snatched the phone from O; sick of listening to their, one sided conversation.

"What's up ma?"

"I want to talk to Nero!"

"That shit not bout to happen, what's up?"

"I want to go home Sacario and they said I need someone to come get me! Let me talk to Nero!" "I said no, I will come get you tomorrow we got some shit we need to talk about." I said ending the call. We went inside and discussed our next step, how we planned on taking Money down. Ali walked in the bar and from entrance you could tell he was pissed; he ordered a drink before he spoke even a hello to us.

"Look I can't keep covering yo fuckin ass. You say you a fuckin king, but you act like a fuckin child." He looks in my direction and instantly he has my attention, "My nigga get yo ass beat in here, we brothers, but never forget I can..,"

"Nigga all you can do is take my advice, and here is some really good shit. Never trust a soul that don't have our blood in they veins, and even our blood can be tainted." He looked at Dinero and snatched his drink as the waitress walked over to our table. He downed the drink slammed it on her tray and shot her a harsh look. "Keep them bitches coming;" he ordered directing his attention back on me.

"That nigga Money shot my nephew. Yo wife trying to kill herself, and I am at my job trying to figure out what bitch snitched on you , and not so much that they could be contemplating bringing yo dumb ass in this week?"

"Fuck you mean, no bitch know shit about me?" I assured my brother pouring myself a glass of Ace, when I looked over at Dinero, he was slumped over the table inhaling the white powder that we made our living from. I sighed, because I knew for a fact that he had been off that shit for years, what the fuck was going on with my brother. Ali finally looked over at Dinero and caught a glimpse of him rubbing his nose, and his eyes widened. He stood to his feet pushing the table over, "Fuck is wrong, with y'all? Is it ok that I put my life on hold to cover yo asses and you just continue to be reckless?" All eyes was on Lee and so was I, I stepped into his space, and looked him over. Our chest on the verge of touching, "Nigga no one is asking you to give up shit, in fact if that's what you feel you have been doing remove yo-self. Nobody need a disloyal bitch in they're shit."

"Fuck you Killa! Disloyal." He lifted his shirt showing the tattoos we all had gotten as teens. Death before Honor Loyalty and brother hood with each other's names. It was the unspoken bond that we had, before we found out that we shared a blood line, and here I was questioning my brother who had never deserted me. "Nigga I'm trying to keep yo ass out a grave and my

233

nephew out of jail, and this nigga out our supply." We both looked at Dinero the waitress walked over to us informing us that people were listing handing, Ali another drink. He downed it tossed a stack of money in the air, and turned to leave, "guess its money over family too Killa." I sucked my teeth curious of who my brother was talking about. That had to be the last thing on my mind; I had to get my family back right. First job was getting my wife, yeah it was after ten at night, but it was time to get the house in order, only then could I call myself a king once I was sure that I had the right Queen, and she was playing her role.

I gathered my brother dropped him off at his house and had Lee meet me at Nero house.

I got Nero in the house and thought it was odd that Kym and the baby weren't home, but shit who was I to judge when my house was just as messy. I hopped in the car with Lee who had a bottle of sprite in his hand, and I was sure that it was truly filled with 1800.

"Look bro I know you cover my ass, I am grateful, but I'm not kissing no nigga—

"Nigga I—

"Hear me out" I said tired of us cutting each other off.

"I need to make shit right with my wife, and then we can get rid of the dead weight. Ali nodded. I assured my brother that I was King and I had shit under control.

"What about Olivia"

"She business"

"You sure bout that, because , she hit me saying she having yo kid and she sick of you, either you step up or she gone make trouble. On top of that I got to go in the office and find out who the fuck is the informant that snitching on you, Nigga its time you realized why we blessed you with the name Killa, no witnesses, ever! He said going in his waist band handing me Beretta. No words needed to be said, as I exited the truck and hopped in my ride. I watched as my brother pulled off and I started towards my car. As soon as I got in I stared at the gun and wondered could I be the same nigga I was fifteen years ago, or was I to hell bent on being the family man. I started the car and made my way towards the hospital thinking of my past.

Flashes of the nigga Silk in my head. Truth he was the only father I knew, and to find he had crossed me and wanted to me dead, all because of my last name, I wanted to make his life hell. Although Dinero had decapitated that nigga, why should he have a blood line, when he had damn near took out mine. To think that the bitch I love the most was the seed of a man that I killed, the nigga I trusted to kill my enemies and guard my family also, a blood line I vowed to kill. Maybe Saint had figured out that Lanya was his sister and was plotting against me. At this point I truly couldn't be sure, all I knew is that, it was time to clean house, a round table would be the best way to see who still belonged in my army. We had one years ago, and it brought the demise of my best friend, was I sure that I could, deal, with another loss like that, Was I ready, for Saint to know the role I played in his life. My wife to know I kept more secrets from her." I hopped out the car and rushed in side St John's hospital. I was ready to run my hands through Nya's hair and make love to her. I needed her pussy to relax my mind. My head spent, when the nurse told me she had just been checked out, by her Lawyer. My first thought was the bitch Olivia had got brave. I pulled my phone, and stormed out the hospital, dialing Olivia, when I see a ghost, well at least he would be when I was done with him. Nigga had his hands in my wife, hair and her head on his chest.

"Fuck is this shit I say, pulling the gun Lee had just given me from my waist band. David raised his hands and took two steps back.

"Sacario what are you doing, this is David, you know the nigga who got your brother out of jail.

"I know who the fuck boy is, clearly he has no idea who I am" The nigga looked me up and down, trying to prove he had heart, but my hand was itching to prove that you, don't touch, what belongs to Killa. Lanya marched over to me pushing the gun against her chest. "You gone kill someone? Kill me Killa! Take my life, I'm sick of yo—I placed my hand over her mouth with my free hand lowering my gun. I looked the Nigga David over one last time Nodded at him and tossed my wife over my shoulder, her mouth and become too much, and it was time to see that I was still the nigga she loved.

≈ ≈ ≈ ≈ ≈ ≈

I took my wife to the Detroit Marriott at the Renaissance Center. I got the most expensive suite they had to offer, and carried her in, She had fallen back to sleep on the drive down town. I undressed her, and laid beside her stroked her stomach remembering that I couldn't make love to her. I pulled her into my arms and kissed her lightly. For the first time in a long I felt whole as a man. I closed my eyes finally sleeping.

The sound of my phone ringing broke my sleep checking to see that Lanya was still by my side I climbed out my bed grabbed my phone from my jeans and walked into the bathroom.

"So you gone call me, hang up then just ignore the fact that I been trying to get in touch with yo ass."

"What you not gone do is talk to me like some bitch nigga Olivia, I told yo ass we was over, I meant that shit. You need to watch ya tone and yo words talking to nigga like me."

"So you just say fuck me, and yo son, Yo only son, you know that—,"

"Bitch my son name is Sacario Alton Jr." She paused and sucked her teeth.

"But you told me that yo wife didn't know if you were the father—," I cut her off again.

"Bitch what I told you was that someone was black mailing my wife, and I needed to find out who, and how to handle that shit, again you don't get you are my fuckin lawyer nothing more." I reminded the bitch, I could hear it in her breathing that didn't please her.

"Sacario you may fail to recall I know all your secrets," I laughed this dumb bitch thought she was smart, I was smarter.

"Fuck you want Olivia?"

"I have a room two doors away I want you in it in the next ten minutes, and yo dick in my mouth." The fuck this bitch was crazy no one knew where the fuck I was and this bitch had not only found out, but was now throwing threats like I was the type punk ass nigga that fall for that shit. I was gone oblige and give the bitch one last fuck, but trust her last nut was gone be the death of her. I walked out the bathroom, looking at Lanya standing by the window nothing covered her body and her hair sat in the middle of her back, I had never seen anything so sexy in my life.

"You know sixteen years and we have never been on vacation, or even had a honeymoon." Lanya said and I could hear the sadness in her voice.

"Yeah I know babe," I walked behind her wrapping my arms around her, pulling her soft body to me, I could smell her sweet hair and fell in love all over again.

"Nya I'm gone do better on my life baby." She tried to pull away and I turned her around to face me lifting her chin I gazed in her eyes.

"Nya I love you."

"So you say, but you cheat and lie then you yell, you no different from any man that I have been with." I could do nothing, but laugh knowing how far from the truth that was, but Nya was truly feeling that was a true statement.

"That's yo word ma?" She pulled away and I tossed her to the bed. I sat beside her and placed her on my lap.

"Listen to me Lanya, you my wife. There is no other woman that can take yo place, but trust when you do the shit you do; I do the shit I do." She laughed and rolled her eyes at me.

"So you cheat on me, because I do what exactly Sacario, not love you, because I waited seven years for you, not hold you down, because when niggas stripped me, of what I built with you, I rebuilt it and gave it to you the day you came home. Disloyal, because I am fucking a nigga on the daily to stay in the loop, so what could I be doing that's not good enough Sacario, I been yo queen since day one, and you still play me like I'm the Pawn." I had to laugh because Nya had proven to be my everything, she was even fuckin Jayce for Dinero to see what he was up to. What she didn't get is I needed more from her. I needed the passion she once gave, I needed my wife not just another solider.

"Nya this is our problem," I lifted her body, on my lap facing me. I cupped her breast in my hand and kissed each breast. Her body was so perfect it made it hard for me to function. I slipped one breast in my mouth, the other I ran my hand over pinching her nipple loving the way she moaned and her body shook as she sat on my lap.

"Stop Cario I can't," she pushed away damn near falling on the floor. I grabbed her placing her back on my lap. "See that's the fuck shit I mean. You mine. Whatever I wanna do to you I can do! That's why I cheat Nya. I be willing to give you my all my everything, fuck I gave you my name—,"

"Then you took it back."

"Damn Nya I took it back to protect you, you know your role, and you always knew you were mine. I'm sick of the living apart, the fighting and all the other bull shit."

"All yo choice Cari."

"My choice aye, well tonight is the last time we sleep apart, tonight is the last time my dick gone be hard and you say no! So whatever secrets you keeping now is the time to speak on." Dinero had told me about her stepfather and the lie he had told her, now it was her turn. The sound of my phone filled the room, and that was now Lanya's focus.

"Who is that yo bitch?"

"Nah you my bitch, so talk to me!"

"I'm no one's bitch, Killa." I smiled kissing her lips. I slid my tongue in her mouth and began to rub her smooth ass. I just wanted to plunge inside what I knew to be the best pussy in the world. She sat on my lap grinding as my wood tried to break free from my sweat pants. I could hear her heart race, and her hands shake as her mouth allowed light moans to escape. She pulled my man hood out lifted her body and slid on top of me.

"Ah agrr oh God." She cried, clawing her sharp nails into me and laughed.

"You sure," I asked and she nodded her head and slowly moved up and down on my dick. I could feel her pussy getting beyond wet as she dug into me with her claws and my phone continued to ring. I was sure it was

Olivia, but I didn't care I was back inside my baby, and nothing could take me away. Nya fucked me till we both came and she passed out on the bed. I wanted to hold her, but I knew I had business to handle. I kissed Nya, realizing she still hadn't told me about the bitch nigga that had raped her. She had been using that same trick for fifteen years when she was avoiding something, and again, it had worked. I showered and put on my jogging pants, wife beater and Jay's and headed to Olivia's room, my phone in my hand.

Chapter 24

The Lying Game

Kym

"...What'cha gonna do?

When you can't say no?

When her feelings start to show?

Boy, I really need to know

And how you gonna act?

How you gonna handle that?

What'cha gonna do when she wants you back?..."

Mya case of the ex was blasting in my head, my heart was pounding and tears were so close to escaping my eyes. I just knew that if I didn't do what Twan wanted I would lose it all. My house, cars and even the money, were all at risk. I would walk away, but Twan would tell Nero things that I knew would take him away from me, and it was no chance that he would allow me to keep our son. The worse thing is, Dinero may had forgiven me for my past, but the shit that Twan had been forcing me to do lately, it was no turning back. I took a deep breath and looked beside me on the night stand picking up the gold plated mirror. A pile of coke sat on the mirror and a blade. I thought of just slashing my wrist, and just looking at my reflection, I should have. I hated coming face to face with who I was becoming.

Not just because I could see my beauty fade, and I was using more cover girl to hide behind, but the person I had become, the longer I spent with Twan. He handed me a glass of clear liquid, I was sure it was Vodka, but I didn't care at this point I downed it tossed the glass on the bed, snorted another line of coke and handed Twan the mirror. When coke hits you, your body doesn't know if it's hot or cold your heart races but your body is calm. You want to laugh at everything at the same time you wanna scream. It's the craziest feeling you will ever have. It's also the best. That and the Vodka had me amped. Sitting up in the bed I got on all fours and crawled over to Twan, I wasted no time pulling his dick from his pants and placing it in my mouth. It wasn't as big as Dinero's so I had no problem deep throating it. He pushed my head deeper down on it, and I just went faster and harder letting moans come out my body as my pussy, began to juice. I reached down dipping my fingers in my cream. Once I was sure they were wet I ran my finger over my clit looking up at Twan enjoy what I knew I would get killed for giving away. He busted in my mouth and pushed me to the bed. I swallowed his sour juice and spread my legs inviting him in. He stroked his dick, then started to push inside me and I lost my breath. "Condom T," I remind him that I was still Dinero's and he rolls his eyes going inside me raw. God O was gone to kill me when he found out. I knew that it was only a matter of time.

After sex for some reason Twan wanted to hold me like I was his, God how did I get myself in this place.

"T I got to go pick up my son and get home to my husband, its after 10 at night."

245

"I know what time it is, yo husband, I don't see no fuckin ring, and that nigga will never love you like I do."

"Twan you don't know how to love," I tell him sitting up to get out the bed. He grabs me and slams me to the bed, his hand around my throat as he squeezes. "Bitch don't ever question my love, it was never a day I didn't wonder why my WIFE didn't come see me. It wasn't a day I didn't miss you. And I have fuckin loved you since we was fourteen years old Kymberly Kamya Craig." Twan was so pissed, he was using my full name. He bent to kiss my lips. "See you forget even if that nigga say he wants to marry you, that yo dumb ass is already married. I am yo husband, don't you fuckin forget that." He fell to the side of the bed and slipping his arms around my body and kissed my neck, as he went to sleep, that's when the tears fell. I Closed my eyes thinking how lucky Nya was that she had escaped and here I was thinking that Dinero was my new start and Twan was there holding me in my past. I laid back in his arms listening to the sound of Pusha T Sweet Serenade, and knew that was Dinero calling looking for me. Yeah it was a matter of time before he found out, if he didn't already know.

Lanya

Wow did this nigga really think that his dick game was gone knock me out to the point that I forgot that he was just on the phone agreeing to meet some bitch in this very hotel. How dare he preach to me about pushing him away and he go cheat. He better be glad that I had a rapid HIV test before I left the hospital, while he was digging in me like he was looking for something. Now he was creeping to be with another bitch, let me find out it's black Barbie and they both dead. I thought watching him close the door. I jumped out the bed and slipped on my jeans and bra and pulled his gun from under the bed. I hid it under the bed, the minute I heard him ending the call. That was why I was standing by the window when he came out the bathroom. I didn't bother putting on shoes I ran out the door to see Sacario walking into a room. Bitch was on the same floor as we were on. This nigga really was feeling like a king, well I was about to de throne this nigga. I thought of just knocking, but said forget it and ran downstairs. I was half dressed in a four star hotel I knew they would have no problem, hurrying to give me a key. I leaned over the desk. Reading the blonde hair beauties name tag. She was staring at me and I didn't care. Shit I was sure that everyone was looking at the black girl in four hundred dollar jeans no shoes and a sheer black bra. "Room 1014 please." The woman smiled at me and looked at the computer. "Your ID please?" I stepped back allowing her to take a look at me. I was about to turn around and show her my ass when I remembered the gun I had placed back there.

"Name," I rubbed my hands together wondering who he was with, praying that it wasn't Olivia and I would say the name and be wrong. "Ma'am name?"

"Olivia, Olivia Alton." I say and the woman smiles.

"Oh the honeymoon suite, I get it now, Mrs. Alton." She hands me the key and I return the smile. I rushed out of the lobby. I jumped in the elevator just as it was closing. The man standing beside me couldn't take his eyes off me, as I made it to my floor, I was sure that the other man had been looking so hard he had missed his, floor but at this point. I didn't care. I was on a mission I stepped off and as the man tried to follow I turned shot him a look like I would kill him with one touch. He stepped back on the elevator and I made my way to room 1014. I truly didn't know what I was gone say, nor did I know what I would do. I slipped my hand in my pocket pulling his ring and my engagement ring off, I had forgot they were there, and wondered what made me think of them, nonetheless. I held Sacario's commitment in one hand and a key card in the other. I slid the key in the door, and before I could get in good I can hear her moaning begging for him to take his pussy.

"Yes daddy I love you," she cried and I laughed. I pulled the gun and held it both hands as I walked in the room. Bitch was on top of him bouncing, his hands around her waist and I almost lost my lunch.

"Fucked up that a nigga more loyal to the street then he is to the bitch that hold him down when the streets turn they back on him! I guess all that wife shit was bull." I looked at the rings and tossed them to the floor. "Give these to her you already gave her my name."

"Nya," Sacario yelled as I started to walk out tears were in my eyes, but this nigga would get not one more from me.

"Lanya it's not what it look like babe." I hear Sacario moving around and I stand there unable to move.

"Fuck that bitch," I hear Olivia say and I turn no longer fighting tears, my gun pointed directly at her.

"Who yo wife Cario, pick now?" I ask as the bitch stands up, smiling her body uncovered, and her belly stuck out like a score thumb. I lose my footing dropping the gun to the ground. "Nya babe it's not what you think," he says and I want to hear nothing he has to say. I took a deep breath and made my way back to my feet. I didn't care that he had fucked her, all men cheat, I didn't care that he lied all men do, but the fact that another woman was carrying his child. Nikki wasn't enough; he had taken that away from me yet again. I held my empty stomach that he had personally been responsible for leaving it deserted. Sacario, rushed to me trying to console me, but I was beyond that. I pushed him back, and wiped my face.

"I'm fine Killa, I mean Sacario I really am. I have - -," I tripped over my words and every time he tried to touch me I pulled away. "I just need to go home," I turned to face him reaching to hug him. He bent to kiss my neck and I closed my eyes tighter. "Next time I take a bottle of pills let me die." I whispered in his ear pulling away. I smiled and tossed the key card to the floor.

"See you at home Cari." I felt insane as I walked out the door, but that bitch had took enough from me, I be damn if she knew it was killing me.

Kym

A week had passed since I had spent the entire night with Twan and Dinero still was pissed. I stood holding Jay Shawn and watching him dress when he turned and gave me a sick look. "I got business tonight, I want my son in his bed, when I come in."

"And what time will that be?"

"Fuck you mean what time? Whenever my Timberlands hit the fuckin floor, that mean yo ass better be in the house, you understand me?" I rolled my eyes feeling like a child not an equal.

"Fuck you Nero you won't even marry me so why should I stay home and—?"

I never saw his hand coming I just felt every bit of his three hundred pounds.

"Marry you, what you think because you been sucking my dick better and fucking me harder that get you a fuckin ring? A wife knows her place play her role and oh yeah, a wife don't steal two fuckin Kilos of pure coke from they husband, and cost him seventy grand. So when you learn how to do that shit, let a nigga no. Bitch stealing and got half a million in a fuckin off shore account all she got to do is ask." He said walking over to the dresser and putting on his watch. Jay Shawn was kissing my face where his daddy had just hit me, and I felt so weak.

"Nya agreed to meet me for shopping and lunch, can I go?" I asked tears falling from my face.

He looked back and laughed. "Yeah how much you need?" He asked bending to pick up our son. He kissed my face where he had just hit me and I flinched.

"I don't need anything Nero I have a couple of dollars for food and I won't shop." He chuckled tossing a black card on the bed, and walked out the room, I won't lie a bit of relief filled my face as I picked the card off the bed and looked at it. That is until I heard the door slam. I looked up to see Dinero had just taken Jay to his room. Now I was beyond scared. O had hate in his eyes and I was sure that he was gone kill me I sat the card on the nightstand as I stood and began to back away from Dinero the closer he came.

"Now yo ass scared of me, you wasn't scared when you was stealing from me or lying to me. You thought I wasn't gone find out yo ass was using that shit?" He questioned grabbing me and slamming me into the wall. His eyes stared into my soul and I was shaking. "Nero you act like you don't use it too."

"I pay for it Kym."

"And that make it right Nero, I didn't steal it I flushed the first kilo the second one I started, then I flushed, I don't want to do the shit no more babe." I lied and prayed he was buying, my bull. He looked me over and grabbed my hand pulling me into his body. His arms were so warm and safe. "I love you Mami and if you want ya ring ask for that shit, don't go doing dumb shit. I know who my wife is," he went into his pocket. He popped something in his mouth then kissed me. He took my hand stroking his face with it, he then kissed my hand slipping my finger in his mouth and biting down gently. When he pulled my finger from his lips there set the perfect ring. A smile covered my face, fear filled my heart. What the hell did I get myself into? Dinero was really gone to kill me when the truth came to light. I walked over to the bed and fell backwards motioning for Dinero to come over.

"Naw ma I got to meet my brother save it for me." He says and I cross my arms over my chest he walks over to me bend down and kiss my lips. "You love me K?" I shook my head yes watching as Dinero dropped to his knees parting my legs and pushing my panties to the side. I swallowed hard as Dinero bit my clit lightly getting my juices to flow. My body shook, as Dinero ate me like a five star meal. I screamed, cried and even tried to push away, but until I exploded all over Dinero's face I saw no mercy.

"Give my shit away Kym, and you will pray for death." He stood from his knees kissed my lips and walked into the bathroom leaving me in deep thought. I had to talk to Twan I had to end this shit now.

"Alright babe I'm gone." Dinero said and his voice nearly made me jump out of my skin. I sat up looking as Dinero left and back at my ring I was in too deep.

HARDER

a. Physically toughened; rugged.

b. Mentally toughened; strong-minded.

Nothing in life worth having comes easy, Hard is just the start of what is to get harder

Part II enter at your own risk...

Chapter 25:

Fake and Phony

Lanya

I sat in the restaurant looking at my second slice of cake, wondering, why I was forcing myself to eat so much. It had been a week and two days since I found out that Sacario was having another child with another woman. The week had been super crazy. He came home yelling at me, then telling me that he loved me, but I was the bipolar one psh. He took me to city hall and we remarried. His words were to me were you want the name it's yours, My husband was a real dick. I no longer desired to have the name and the ring felt like a leash on my finger. Then to add more to it Kym wanted to meet for lunch. Now she was talking to me like we were best friends. As if she hadn't abandoned me for the last seven years, the seven years I needed her most.

"Lala you hear me?" She says and I snap out my thoughts.

"No I'm sorry," I say it again, I say twisting the two brand new rings that had been placed on my finger. Truthfully they meant nothing to me. The old ones now just a charm on my necklace, Cario had given me last night. I felt as if I was surrounded, by fake people and phony promises. "Lala where are you?" Kym asked and I laughed. I went to cut into her, but I kept my mouth shut. I didn't have the heart to fight I guess I was the fakest of all the people I knew. "Hey sis!" I hear a voice say and Kym stands I turn to look at who was so close to me. Tara? I question as she hugs Kym working her way to me. I stand and hug her. Tara was like my sister in high school. Kym Tara and I were inseparable. We were together so much that people really thought that were sisters. Then suddenly our senior year her father comes take her way and I don't see her God she had changed, but managed to keep the same busted fashion since high school. "What are you doing here?" I asked truly happy to see her.

"Bitch that's what I was telling you," Kym says as Tara sits down. I look at my phone sitting on the table, "one second y'all." I say pressing talk.

"Hello."

"What up little bit what you doing?" Ali asked and for some reason I feel like a school girl. "Having lunch with my sisters."

"Sisters who is that? A group or some shit?"

"No fool Kym and Tara," he laughed.

"Oh I'm a fool now? Alright, I called to congratulate you on getting that name back."

My whole mood changed when he said that and I looked back at my rings. "Oh yeah thanks, um Lee I got to go can I talk to you later?" "Fasho," he said and I ended the call trying to smile, so Kym nor Tara would know how bad I was hurt.

"That was yo husband?" Tara asked and my stomach flipped upside down.

"No I'm married to his brother, anyway bitch tell me what is going on with you?" I say a smile heavy on my face hiding the pain; I guess I had gotten good at that.

≈≈≈≈≈≈

It had been two months and I couldn't bear looking my husband in his eyes. However I played the role. I had no choice, I was still in love with a man that had betrayed me. I won't lie my thoughts at time were to

258

do as my uncles had once asked and turn on him. But I loved him too much, to hurt him despite the fact that he had no problem hurting me. I rolled over removing my head from Sacario's chest. He pulled me back, on top of him. I put a fake smile on my face and pulled myself up. "Morning Birthday boy," I said kissing Sacario's fore head. "Um that's all I get?" He asked me, and I felt sick to my stomach jumping up and running to the bathroom. My heart was racing as I threw up last night's meal. I stood leaning over the sink washing my mouth out and brushing my teeth when Sacario came into the bedroom. He pulled his dick out and began to pee as if I wasn't standing there. This was nothing new for us, however I was still feeling as if he was a stranger, and didn't want to be in the same room with him. "You alright babe?" Sacario ask reaching over me putting soap on his hands and kissing my neck as he washed his hands. I dipped under his arms and walked back into the bed room. I quickly dressed, before he realized I was avoiding his question. I didn't need him to know he had two women pregnant at the same time, and truth was I had no plans on keep our child. Tears filled my eyes every time I thought of another woman giving birth to my husband's child. She would get it all, there child would get to be with him his whole life. My children didn't get that. I hated them both for that. The longer I spent with Sacario, the more I hated him, for giving her all that I ever wanted from him; his love.

I stood in the kitchen cutting my daughters pancakes when Deuce sat down at the table. "Sup ma"

"Hey baby, you want some pancakes?" He laughed and poured himself a glass of juice.

"Sup little bit, you get prettier overnight" He kissed his little sister and took a slice of bacon from her plate.

"Hey she said handing him, another. I loved the relationship my children had with each other.

"Ma I'm hanging wit Jay today." I sighed and placed his plate before him.

"That's fine Sacario, just please make sure to tell yo father happy birthday, and answer yo phone if I call." He nodded his head yes and stuffed his face with pancakes. He chugged his juice and stood from the table wiping his mouth and kissing his sister.

"You need cash?"

"Nah I'm good ma" he says grabbing his hat from the table and walking towards the door. Deuce pauses and walks back to the stairs, "Yo Pops" Sacario walked to the balcony. He was rocking a dark pair of Levis and some Jordan's, he was topless and his chest looked so good covered in tattoos. "Sup nigga, where you going?"

"Mall wit Jay, Happy birthday old man" Sacario laughed and walked down the stairs hugging Deuce. He went in his pocket handing him, the wad of cash he had in his pocket. "Don't buy no cheap shit" Sacario told his son. Deuce nodded and started back out the door. "Yo D give me ten minutes, and you and ya nigga can hang wit me." That's cool" Deuce said leaning against the wall.

"Wow really, if I had asked you to go to the mall with me, you would have rather died." Sacario laughed as he walked in the kitchen smacking my ass. "That's because yo ass nag too much" He kissed my face and took a slice of bacon. His body was pressed against mine and I was becoming so turned on, but we hadn't been having sex, why should anything change now. I turned to face my husband kissing his lips. "Your daughter is watching, and your son is waiting, do you really want birthday sex in the kitchen." He laughed and kissed my neck

"Shit if you was really gone fuck me you could bring yo fine ass up stairs, but you not talking that real shit, so it don't even matter." He kissed my neck and pulled away. "Let me get my shirt nigga and I'll be ready", Sacario told Deuce and ran up the stairs.

I was so damn horny I wanted to run behind him lock the door and let him fuck me till I couldn't move, but instead I got Alyssa up and dressed. I did her super thick, long hair. I grabbed my phone, and pushed myself to keep up my actions.

"Hey Kym, what ya doing?"

"Shit bout to take yo nephew to my moms, what's up." She says

"It's Killa's Birthday, and I have to go shopping for his gift and get the rest of the things for the party tonight. You want to hang?"

"Yeah that sound, fun I will be ready, in about an hour. I ended the call and went to my room dressed, as I slipped into my jeans that were starting feel extremely too tight. I lied across the bed and lying beside me was a sheet paper with a number on it, it was written in Sacario's hand writing. I picked the paper up and slipped it in my pocket. Then zipping, up my jeans. I grabbed my keys purse and slipped on my thigh high boots and was ready to go.

Kym, Alyssa and myself hit the mall, but I knew the gifts I wanted for Cario could not be found here. They had to be pre ordered witch I had done the week I decided to through him, a birthday party at the Boss's Lounge. However I did find nice things for myself and the rest of my family. I was having a great day with Kym, and truly wasn't in a rush for it to end, I got a Text from Tara saying that she would love to see me and I urged her to meet us for lunch, when she got time. Just as I hit send my phone began to ring.

"Hello"

"Hey ma what ya up too" Ali asked in a relaxed tone

"Picking up a few things for tonight," A smile covered my face like a candle had been lit I had an idea.

"Speaking of tonight, do you have a date?" Ali chuckled,

"Man Nya you know I be too busy working to find a date," I could feel the plot coming together in my head, I could introduce Tara and Lee. That would hopefully stop the lustful thoughts I had been having, about him. "Well I may have someone for you, meet me at summer set, in about two hours, I may be able to change all that.

"Man Nya I don't know about all that, you be having them friends, niggas be wanting to wife, I'm to fly for just one woman. He said, and I knew he was lying, but who was I to judge. I ended the call and continued to shop when my text alert went off again. A smile still heavy on my face as I looked at the image that loaded on the unregistered number. My hands began to shake and hot tears fell down my eyes as I felt my heart crumble.

Chapter 26: Real Love

Sacario

Nya had been acting; dry as fuck towards, me however I understood that shit would take time. I assured her that Olivia was not having my child, and all would be right between us. I knew that she still felt a little wary, so I bought us tickets for a cruise, we would leave after my birthday. Now that she was pregnant I wasn't sure that was a great idea, nonetheless I needed to show her that she was the only woman I could ever love.

I laid back in the barber chair a hot rag over my face as I listened to my brothers and sons joke. It felt good to have both my boys together, and for them to be so close filled my heart, even if they didn't know they were kin. I didn't stress it much Lee and I didn't find out till I was 21 and we were still the best of friends, that secret made us closer, than anyone could ever imagine. "Yo nigga so you and the Mrs. back on good terms, or she still acting out. My barber asked. I had to smile, "Man my wife know not to play with me. I run shit in my fuckin house—Ali started to laugh and Dinero just said a simple shid. "Nigga fuck you, and you, Mrs. Alton know who the law-

"Dad, dad" Deuce yelled out.

"Shut up little nigga cuz you know like I know

"What they fuckin know Killa" I hear my wife's voice say. I snatch the towel from my face and sit up. A smile on my face when I look at Lanya's sexy almond color skin diamond shaped eyes and thick frame. I stand up tossing the towel in the chair. All eyes were on me, and I didn't care my baby was looking good as fuck.

"Sup baby, I was just explain to these niggas that you the shit I say placing my hands on her hips. She stepped back and crossed her arms over her chest.

"Fuck you Sacario, you can tell these hoe ass niggas what you, want to, and just make sure you let them know that you are, a two time, low rent, no good fake ass nigga, and for that we done.

"Fuck wrong with you?" I ask grabbing at her, when she reached behind her and pulled a gun from her waist. She aimed it at me causing Dinero and Ali both to get to their feet.

"Yo Nya, put that shit up" Dinero yelled at her she turned to look at him and I placed my hand on the barrow of the gun and snatched it from her. I handed the gun to

Ali who was the closet to me. I stepped closer to her. "Fuck is wrong with you"

"Yo bitch ass, weak fuck nigga I hate you, bum bit—before she could finish I had her up in the air by her throat.

"Pop's," Deuce yelled out and I placed her to the ground.

She grabbed her neck and I stood and looked at her.

"Fuck you Killa, we done, you fuckin hear me" I stepped in her face and pressed my hands in her face pushing, her backwards. "Get the fuck on wit that shit, keep telling you, that fuckin ring mean you mine, and even if you take the bitch off, the minute I bussed in you, I owned you. She pulled away and started to walk towards the door. I was pissed off, however, she was my wife I started to chase her out the door. I grabbed her soon as we got outside her eyes were puffy and red, I knew she had been crying.

"What's up ma talk to me," She turned hugging me I rubbed her back, know this was gone be the longest nine months of my life, Lanya pulled away now my gun was in her face. She held it to her chin, more tears traced her cheeks. "How much Carri, how much I got to love you, what's it gone take, for you to know I can't live without you, is gone take my death, because I will do it. I will blow my brains out to show you that I have always been your, I just can't take the pain. Is loving you not enough" tears rolled down her eyes I reached for the gun and she moved it from her chin cocking it. She took another step back and started to cry. "Mommy I hear my daughter scream." I'm sorry Carri, I'm sorry for whatever I did, just stop hurting me, please" she plead. She was starting to draw a crowd. Ali and Dinero, didn't even know how to act or react in that matter.

"Ma Lyssa watching" Deuce said stepping into my wife. She handed me the gun and fell to her knees. Deuce bent to pick her up. He started to hug his mother and I stepped in handing him the gun I pulled her into my arms.

"Ma I love you, stop acting insane" I say kissing her neck and she push back. She went into her pocket pulling her phone she scanned through it then handed it to me. You love me so much you fuck anything moving, I'm not good enough. You know what you don't want me the next man will, and I will surly give him all you didn't want." She leaned in and laughed in my ear, you know what I'm gone continue to play my role, the party the gifts, but just no this ring means nothing, The child I carry dead I can't with you anymore. She steps back and starts to walk away and pauses. Killa I need yo keys to yo truck so I can take my kids home and get the shit that I need. Nya was talking and I was getting more pissed, by the second. I knew she was mad, but until I looked at the ultrasound photo in her phone did I understand. I really couldn't fight with her, I was still fucking up, and Olivia should have been got rid of that damn baby" I dug in my pocket handing her the keys to my truck as she handed me hers.

"Babe can I please?"

"Fuck you Killa."

"FUCK NYA" she smiled and turned around and looked back at me, "I'm sorry baby it won't happen again, I love you Cari" Nya says her voice dripping of sarcasm. I couldn't even respond I just walked back in the shop and flopped down in the chair.

"Just cut my hair nigga" Ali and Dinero walked in all I could do is, laugh.

"Man fuck y'all I say listening to the two of them mock myself and Nya.

"No fuck you Killa but I love you." Dinero said once again making fun of my situation with my wife.

"What the fuck was that all about?" Ali asked with a raised eyebrow.

"Olivia sent Nya an ultrasound picture. Now I have to go see this bitch take her to the fuckin clinic."

"Fuck the clinic gone do Nya gone kill that bitch," Dinero said rubbing his hands together.

"My wife don't have the heart."

"Shid." they both said in unison making me question if I really knew my wife.

"Hello." Ali says into his phone holding up his hand to silence us from are jokes.

"What up Mrs. Killa, what's that you say you wanna tell me where I can pick my baby brothers balls up at" I gave my brother a blank stare wondering, why my wife was calling him. I always felt they had something going on, but this was confirming it. Ali ended the call and stood to his feet.

"Alight my niggas duty calls, Nya got me on that suicide Mission and You know what happen if you go up against a nigga like lil Killa she pop up at ya hang out and cut ya balls off." Ali joked as he dapped both Dinero and myself and left the shop. I could have pressed the matter,

One being Olivia wilding out, two Money bitch ass still was MIA since the day he shot my son, and I owed him a fuckin bullet.

Money

Stepping back in my spot after, lying low felt good. I was able to really think on how I was gone to take over this game and make heads turn while doing it. I thought for a moment that Lanya was my way in. She knew his game and could school me on the things he did in the game, but when I fell in love with her I was thrown for a loop. She had me feeling like she saw a future for us. That was the only reason I showed up at that hospital, that day. Finding out she had my seed growing inside her made shit all the better. I never meant for shit to go down as they did, and popping little nigga was never part of the plan, but I knew I couldn't in good standing stick around for the back lash. I knew Jayson was safe, after all he was also Killa's son. The one thing that kept my son and I from having the bond I truly wanted with him. However I left Jayson in good hands with my mother, I just needed to regroup. I knew Sacario would be on the hunt for me, I won't lie, but at that time I wasn't ready for him. However I took the two months to build my army, get my connect right outside of Dice Marks. When I stepped back in Detroit Sacario was gone get a real fight. When Jayson

271

told me that Sacario was having a party tonight at his bar I knew that this was the perfect time. What better time could I stunt on this nigga, show that my army was in effect and take his bitch.

I was beyond Pissed to find out that Lanya had killed my baby, and remarried this nigga. All the fuckin stories she had told me, how this nigga lied cheated and even put his hands on her and she runs back to this nigga. That's the definition of a Silly Hoe, nonetheless, by the end of the night, I was gone have the last word.

I hopped in the shower Lanya heavy on mind, I was wondering, if that nigga made her kill our seed, or was she playing me. It didn't matter I thought what was done. I hopped out the shower, dressed in Gucci from head to toe. After making a few calls I knew my game plan. Not even Jay knew I was back home and I wanted to keep it that way. Just as I made my way out the door I got the call from my partner, that I had been waiting for, we had a mole inside the Alton camp and she would be the best assist. Twan and I ended the call, leaving me on cloud nine as I prepared myself for one hell of a birthday party.

Chapter 27: Love at first sight

Ali

I truly didn't get the point of Nya hooking me up, I really never meshed with chicks. I had found the love of my life years ago, she just so happened to also be the love of my brother's life and the mother of his kids. I wasn't the one for these messy hood rat

chicks. They always either was stuck on that gold digging, tip or couldn't deal with the fact that I was a cop. It had gotten 100 times worse once I left DPD and joined the FBI task force against crime. In Addition I had change my last name to Alton, My adoptive mother, was kind of hurt, not my pops he was good with it. Nevertheless I agreed to meet the chick; Nya didn't hang around ugly chicks so this should be interesting.

I pulled up at Sumer set mall ready to meet this chick, that I just knew would take my breath away, and when I walked into the Gucci store, I was breathless. Nya was sitting, on a leather chair a glass of what hope was juice in her hand and she was wearing this short black dress with boots all the way up to her thigh. Her legs were crossed seductively so that tiny piece of flesh was showing, just enough to make me wonder if she had on any panties. The closer I got the harder my dick got.

"Sup baby girl" I say extending my arms for Lanya, she sits her glass on the side table a smile covers her face and she springs to her feet. She jumps in my arms and her body feels so good. I lick my lips as I hold her in my arms and I know she is feeling what I do. However she pulls back, and pauses as we come eye to eye, I can't help it bending down and kissing her lips. She slips her warm tongue in my mouth and my dick swells.

"Ummmhum" I hear Kym clear her voice and Nya pushes back. I wipe my mouth and Nya walks away. She lays her head on Kym's shoulder then laugh and Kym waves.

"Sup big Lee, how you bro?" Kym say and I shake my head.

"What up baby sis." Truly hope she don't think I'm worried bout word getting to my brothers, I have killed niggas bigger than her and got away with it, what was another bitch. "What up mama I'm here what you got for me I ask Nya taking the glass from her hand and sipping it.

"Its white grape juice chill" she says still smiling hard as fuck from the kiss we just shared. "Tara I hear Kym yell running to hug a tall yellow chick with freckles. Won't deny that baby girl was thick as snow tires, but the bitch was busted. She had thick ass red dry looking hair. And she was rocking a pair of leggings a long ass sweater and what looked like sketcher gym shoes. I shook my head at Nya before she even started to intro us.

"Tara this is my brother in law Ali, Ali this is Tara." Lanya said walking over to me wrapping her hands around my waist.

"Nice to meet you." I said nodding my head.

"Nya let me holla at you" I walked Nya over to the dressing rooms and cocked my head to the side.

"She look like what I fuck with really, or you giving me bull shit, because you want me?" She sucked her teeth and hit my shoulder. "Damn nigga you sure are cocky" She says not denying that she wanted me as bad as I wanted her. "Look Lee she not top shelf, but nor was I when I got wit Cario, give me a couple hours, she'll be A-1 by tonight that's my word"

"That's ya word, well Brown and Gold is what I'm wearing tonight make that bitch match my fly we got a go, but if not, I'm leaving her at the door step" I looked down at my buzzing phone and answered it handing Lanya, my black master card. We hugged one last time, and I was out the door.

Lanya

Ali was looking good as fuck and his lips were as soft as a down pillow. Damn I was really in love with Sacario, because that kiss should have moved mountains, but all I could think is I love my husband. However I think that Lee was right part of the reason, I wanted him to meet Tara was because she didn't hold candle to me. The other reason was Kym had been hard pressed on hooking her up with someone so that we could all be as close as we use to be, little did she know nothing in this world could change the fact that my best friend turned her back on me not once but twice. I didn't do that three strike shit.

"So that's the third brother? Tara asked as we sat down for lunch."

"Yeah what you think?"

He fine as hell, but it looked like he had his eye on someone else she said. Taking a glass of water from the waitress hand. "I don't know what the fuck you talking about" Kym gave me a side eye and I smiled.

Lunch then a ton of shopping, the beauty shop, nails done legs waxed, Ali was sure to flip when he saw the bill from Tara. Add on the three thousand dollar Versace dress and the eight hundred dollar Gucci shoes. Hell that was nothing compared to what I racked up on Sacario's card. I really didn't need any thing, but my dress and his suit, but I was so mad at that nigga that I was gone make him pay.

≈≈≈≈≈≈

We got home a little after 8 and Tara and Kym both decided that it would be best to dress at my house and let Lee and Dinero pick them up there. I didn't mind, however I knew that Sacario was gone to be in a mood. I dragged the tons of packages into the house, and yelled for my son. He and Jayson rushed down stairs both kissing me. Jayson had been spending more nights than a few at our house and I rather enjoyed it. He was a good kid, and I couldn't deny he looked just like Ali, maybe Dinero either way, I didn't get how no one could see how much he and Deuce looked alike. I handed the boys the things I had bought for them, and began to go through the things I had bought. The sound of the door slamming startled me.

"Sup Kym," Sacario said I stood to see him look at Tara.

"Babe that's Tara, Tara this handsome man is my husband Sacario. I greeted him with a hug and a kiss on his face. "Hey baby can we talk" Sacario asked wrapping his strong arms around me and I felt so weak, however I knew I had to continue to play my role. "Yeah babe, down here or up in the room, I asked running my hand over his stomach.

"Um ma that feel good" he grabbed my hand pulling me up the stairs. I put a huge smile on my face and allowed him to guide me into our bedroom. He closed the door forgetting he asked to talk. He placed his lips on my neck and his hands on my hips; damn you make my dick hard. "You forgive me" I pulled away and rolled my eyes "Talk Cari."

"You can't still be mad Nya."

"That bitch still having yo fuckin baby?"

"You know she is, but—,"

"No buts Sacario we have nothing to say to each other, I'm not that side bitch. You go head be with her, after tonight my wifely duties are done." I said taking my wedding band off leaving my engagement ring on, just for show. I tossed the band at his feet grabbed my house phone off the base and started towards my walk-in closet.

"Hey love is it ok I stay a few nights at your house?" I spoke into the phone knowing Sacario was listing. "Nya" Sacario yelled following me. I began gathering his clothes, for tonight placing them neatly on the bed continuing my phone call.

"You don't fuckin hear me talking to yo ass?" Sacario rips the phone from my hand and tosses to the floor.

"Cut it out Cario" I yell picking the phone up and placing it on the base. Look we have a party to get to, I remind him going into the bathroom cutting the shower on. "Are you coming? I yell for my husband and he stands in the door. So we not together, but we taking showers together?" I laughed and began to shower. I know I was trying to play super bitch, my heart was hurting, and I needed my husband to love me, since he couldn't I was gone to find someone who could, I dint care if it met that I would have to sleep around to do so. Sacario got in the shower behind me. His hands wrapped around my body and I was so tempted to rest my head on him and just have a good cry, but I had promised myself, that Sacario and I were over. We showered, without so much of a touch. I dried my body oiled down and slipped into my thong I could see Sacario looking at the thin piece of lace in-between my ass. I smiled giving him a show. Finally I grabbed my clothes and walked down stairs. Kym and Tara were dressed and looking good. I stood going through packages trying to decide if I was gone to wear the dress I had laid out or the one I just bought. The door opened and I heard Dinero and Ali walk in the house. I didn't give a fuck that I didn't have clothes on, maybe it would be good if the world saw what I was working with clearly my husband could give a fuck less.

"Damn ma you looking good as fuck."

"Thank you daddy," I hear Kym and Dinero and I can't help but laugh and get jealous at the same time.

"Damn, ma you got a nigga feigning can we go upstairs?"

"No Nero it took all day to get ready."

"So you telling yo man no."

"No baby I'm just asking my husband to wait till we get home, so I can suck his dick how I really want to."

"Yeah I like that," Dinero said and again I gag.

I can feel eyes on me so I turn to see Ali look my body over as he spins Tara pretending he's looking her over.

"Damn ma you looking like a million bucks."

"It cost bout that much," I say to Ali as I slip on my black and red dress and walk over to Kym to zip me up. I placed my black diamond drop earrings in my ear and adjusted my necklace. I didn't care if no one else thought I looked good.

"Where the fuck yo husband?" Dinero ask.

"Nigga you know he dress like a bitch." Ali answered and they share a laugh.

"Fuck y'all" Sacario says walking downstairs, he looked so good in his Gucci tux, I could smell the 212 coming off him and instantly was wet. "Thanks babe," Sacario says kissing my face showing off his brand new audemars piguet watch.

"Damn, that's what yo wife bought you for yo cake day?" Ali questioned and Sacario just smiled.

"See babe that's how the hell you give gifts" Dinero says to Kym as we walk out the door.

We stepped into a black limo, and I look back at my house hoping the choice I was making were the right ones. I did love my husband, but I could see myself become someone I wasn't.

Sacario

I stood on the stairs looking at my wife, I won't lie I prayed to God if he gave me one more chance, I would do right by her. My wife had really stepped it up for me and all I could think about was from day I stepped out that cell I have played her dirty. Lanya reached for my hand and rested her head on my arm as we stepped in to a Rolls Royce limo. I won't deny I was impressed.

We pulled up to the Boss's lounge it looked like a Hollywood premier, from the red ropes at the entrance to the red carpet and photo screen. When my wife did something she did it big. We walked in she held on to me so tight I couldn't help but laugh.

"It's perfect babe I love it—she put her hand over my lips and walked away just as soon as no one was looking. I really couldn't figure my wife out, she was up and down, like a roller coaster, but I couldn't let that stress me. I made my way to VIP with my brothers and laid back.

"Yo my nigga wifey out did herself, Ali said raising his glass to Nya I just nodded and poured me a drink. I was scooping out the whole bar when I spotted Nya, she was sitting at the bar with a glass in her hand. Damn was she really gone get drunk with my seed in her belly. I stood making my way down to the bar, taking the glass from Nya's hand I take a sip and shoot her a fucked up look. I sit the glass behind the bar and rip her off the stool.

"What are you doing, Carri?"

"Fuck you doing, you having my baby!"

"Nigga I told you long as that bitch knocked up I'm not having shit" She pointed her finger to the table by the door Olivia sat with a drink in her hand. She had a smile on her face as random niggas sent her drinks; all I could do is sigh. I looked at Nya and tears spilled down her face. "Babe let me get rid of her"

"No fuck it Carri you just want to tell her to put her drink down, and she waiting so go" Nya said noticing that Olivia was looking our way. I sucked my teeth and walked over to Olivia she stood and wrapped her arms around me. She kissed my face and I pulled back and looked at my wife.

"I lifted her drink and smelled it, I didn't even realize how hard Nya was looking until she was no longer in my sight. "Baby its just juice, I thought you didn't care."

"Man I don't Liv, you need to go?"

"No it's my man's birthday, happy birthday baby"

"My wife is flipping out, and you know that we just business so, go.

"Really you want me to go Sacario, all the secrets I know. Don't forget I know when where and how yo coke is shipped—I grabbed her throat and I had to remind myself where I was. I released her and grabbed her hand twisting it behind her back.

"I pray I don't have to remind you on who the fuck I am." She tried pulling away, but by this time I was pissed as fuck. "Last time this baby a no go I tell you one more time, you don't wanna think what I'm gone do. I warn her pushing her down to the booth and walking back towards the VIP, I felt someone grab my arm and I turned my head to feel lips touch mine. I lost my guard and began to return the kiss when I heard someone clear their throat.

I turned to see my wife behind me.

"See bitch I told you he would be back," Janet said and I dropped my head looking at the defeated look on Nya's face. I went to grab her and she ran towards the back door, "Fuck is you doing here Jan?"

"She with me nigga" I knew my ears were deceiving me when I saw Money standing next to Jan. He wrapped his arms around her waist and I laughed,

"Nigga you sure like my left overs,"

"Nigga shit better the second day any way," Money say and I step into his space and Ali grabs me. "Yo wife looking for you," I looked at Money with an ice cold stare and walked away with my brother not completely taking my eyes off that nigga. "I want this nigga bodied by the end of the night" I whisper to my brother. I was way past sick of lying low while niggas acted like my name wasn't Sacario Killa Alton. I pulled away from Lee scanning the room, for Nya, when Ali nodded his head at the office and I started up the stairs. I walked into my office and smiled looking at my wife sitting on top of the desk.

"Lock the door" she says and I lick my lips looking at Nya's thick body. She is perfection. I lock the door and walk over to my desk. I uncross her legs and step in between her thighs. She looks away, and I grab her face forcing her to look at me. I pull her bottom lip in my mouth and bite down. Nya pulls away and wraps her legs around my waist.

"Thought you were mad?"

"Thought you wanted birthday sex?"

"Shit I do" I tell her pulling her ass to the end of the desk and slipping her tongue in my mouth. She pulled back and I cut my eyes at her. "Fuck you doing Nya if—she silenced me placing her lips on mine. Her hands ran up my shirt and her legs lifted wrapping around my back. Her pussy was so hot I could feel it through my pants. Those slowly began to fall as Lanya moved her hands quickly, I didn't have to do anything, as my wife undressed me.

"Damn babe"

"You got a condom?' she asked in between kisses" and I stepped back, this bitch was trying me now.

"For what?" I asked pulling my dick out and rubbing it on her wet pussy.

"Wait Cari my dress" she yelled lift her dress over her head and kissing my neck as I slipped my pipe inside her.

"Yes" she moaned, like she had hit the jack pot I laughed going deeper and harder.

"Am I still yours? Am I daddy?" Nya whined and I went deep and hard.

"You love me Killa, do you" she asked tears running down her face as she locked her legs tighter around me." Her pussy was so wet and good, I found myself moaning, with her.

Lanya's juices were warm, and ran like a faucet. I was never a minute man, but she always knew how to get every drop out of me. I pulled out of her planting kisses on her neck to thank her for the work she had put in, when she dropped to the floor and slipped my dick in her mouth tasting her juices. I ran my hands through her hair and tried to prevent my dick getting hard again.

An hour in my office with my wife had me tired and unsure that I really wanted to go back to the party. Nya walked out the bath room; she had her purse in one hand and phone in the other hand.

"Yeah I'm on my way" she says into the phone and I stand up from my chair and grab her.

"Where you going? I looked at my watch and was really pissed 145 in the morning and she think she leaving this bar. Lanya pulled away walking over to my safe she opened it and quickly went inside. She slammed 3 boxes on the table and gave me an ice stare. Enjoy yo hoes Sacario. She said walking out the office. I glanced down at the nice size boxes and wondered what was inside, but that would have to wait I rushed to follow my wife when I see her talking to Olivia. I nod my head for my brothers Dinero and Ali waste no time coming to my side Saint was in tow. However Nya moved faster and was out the door before we got the front of the bar.

"Fuck happened" Nero asked looking at me like he was mad.

"Man she acting like Nya the brat again I explained. I watched Ali and Saint both roll their eyes and I smirked. I hit Saint on the back of his head and shot Lee a look.

"Nigga go follow my fuckin wife make sure she go home, and if she don't I wanna know where the fuck she at. I told Saint walking to the Bar for a drink.

Lanya

I had called David and told him I was on my way, but after talking to him, I really didn't know if I should go to a hotel, until I could get divorce papers drawn up. Sacario had pushed me too far, and I had broken. I wanted him to hurt as bad as I did, but at the same time I just wanted it to be over. I grabbed my bag out the back seat and started towards David's porch.

"If he don't answer in two minutes I go to a hotel" I said out loud ringing the doorbell. As soon as I heard the Ding dong I was ready to turn around, when David pulled me in his arms, and I felt my body go numb. He took me into his arms and carried me into his home I never paid any mind how strong he was, he was a very handsome man, just not a man I would ever look twice at. I was addicted to bad boys and he was far from the type of man that could breathe fear into me, and I needed a man that could handle me. Nonetheless I was in David's arm and his lips were on my neck. He worked his way to my lips and turned my head. I was still married, and kissing was worse than cheating in my book. David got the point, however he didn't stop his pace carrying me upstairs and into his bedroom, I had no time to react as he undressed me. I wanted to stop him, but at the same time this was my pay back. Finally I could pay Sacario back, for all the pain he had put me through. My mind was racing as David's hands roamed, and before I knew it I felt penetration. My eyes bugged just a bit, before I realized this isn't what I wanted. It felt so good, to be wanted to the magnitude David wanted me, but I belonged to Killa and my husband was crazy, I feared what he would do to David if he found out.

When David was finished I rested on his chest still thinking of my husband as he ran his soft hands through my hair. Even his touch was different from Carri. Why I compared the two I didn't know I just knew that the more he touched me the more I wanted my husband. David drifted off to sleep, so I picked up his shirt from the floor and crept down stairs. I sat on the couch and opened my purse pulling my phone. I noticed the sun was beginning to come up. Looking at my phone to see 49 missed calls and just as many voice mails I was ready to scream.

"Hey Kay what you doing" I asked Kym who sound completely groggy.

"Nya its 6 30 I'm in the damn bed with my man, what are you doing, where are you?"

"I'm with David, but you can't tell Cario, promises"

"I promise she said and I prayed she would keep her word.

"Where are my kids?"

"They wit Killa I guess," She said and I sighed.

"Well I'm safe call me lata" I told her and she ended the call before I could.

"Just as I was placing my phone back in my purse it rang. I quickly answered it.

"Hello" I whispered

"So I have to call yo ass blocked we some fuckin kids! You walk out on my birthday! Fuck you at?"

"I'm safe Killa"

"That's not what I asked yo ass! I said where the fuck are you Lanya?"

"I'm safe and I will come back for my kids when I get a place.

"Nah, you abandoned them, so stay yo ass where you lay. All yo accounts dead and I'm filing for full custody of our kids.

"You wouldn't!"

"You coming home?"

"I can't"

"Why, somebody got you?"

"No I can't stay with a nigga who don't love me," Tears fell down my eyes and I started to shake

"Fuck you mean don't love you! Bitch all I do is for you, don't love you? You my fuckin world, you my heart I'm here dying without you, and you talking that fly shit, man bring yo ass home.

"No Carri"

"Baby I'm sorry I will fix it all, but don't make me live without you!"

"I can't Sacario" I told him trying to catch my breath

"Fuck you mean you can't Lanya? You my damn wife baby come home.

"No Killa"

"Yeah you remind me of who I am, but clearly you have no idea who Killa is, so allow me to introduce him. Bring yo ass home, or leave with what you came with. No cash no kids' house cars nothing Nya.

"Killa that's my shit—

"No that's my shit you my wife, you a law student, and this is why you would never pass the fuckin Bar we stay in Michigan, I am the sole provider, sole meaning everything is mine and I give you what I want you to have. Now bring yo ass home"

"Fuck you Killa" I cried out tossing my phone to the floor, falling beside it tears pouring down my face.

"Baby what's wrong David asked lifting me from the floor and carrying back upstairs. He dried my eyes and promised me that I would never want for anything, that he would make sure I got my kids, and he would love me better. I know the first time we used a condom, but this time I was sure he didn't even attempt to. I felt his warm cum run down my ass as he continued to make promises, of a better life for me.

I woke up to my phone blaring in my ear. I sat up grabbing my phone. I looked to the side of me to see David was not insight.

"Hello" I yelled into my phone

"Ma" My 16 year old said.

"Hey baby"

"Ma, Lyssa crying when you coming home?"

"Soon baby, where is your father?"

"He right here, fuck is you at" Sacario said and I couldn't speak.

"Nya you had ya fun bring ya ass home."

"Hey baby, brought you some food" David says walking into the room, and my eyes get big as quarters.

"Fuck is that Nya, please don't make me kill somebody"

"Sacario we will talk tomorrow I am about to go back to bed." I tell him ending the call tossing my phone to the bed and walking into the bathroom. I climbed into the shower, when David walked in.

"Baby you ok" he asked and I wanted to scream.

"I'm gone let you take your shower he says and I smiled closing the shower door back.

I stepped out of my warm shower to the sound of loud music, and doors slamming. David stayed in a nice area, so I couldn't understand who would be so disrespectful; it was when I heard the voice I froze in one spot.

Chapter 28 Song cry

Sacario

Lanya was pissing me off, if she fucked another nigga they both was dead. I said loading my second hammer. I had called both my brothers, and after Dinero put his foot down Kym told him where Nya was. I had been with this woman sixteen years and she still didn't know who the fuck I was, she was about to find out. I thought tucking my gun down my pants and holstering the other.

"Deuce, get ya sister feed her, and take her to the mall or some shit. When y'all done, go over your Uncle Lee house, me and yo mom need alone time." I tell my son and he shoot me a side eye and sucks his teeth.

"Don't hit my mom," Deuce says to me and I step in his space.

"Who you talking to Sacario?"

"Pops I know you and my mom's beefed out, but don't hit her!" He says and I admire his heart.

"Deuce that's my wife."

"That's my mom."

"Keep in mind, who the fuck I am."

"Who are you?" My son says crossing his arms over his chest and looking at me cocky as hell.

I sucked my teeth, raised my fist and punched him in his stomach.

"Yo fuckin father, go do what the fuck I said!" I told him as he bent over trying to catch his breath.

I pulled up in front of lawyer nigga house, my brothers arrived seconds behind me. I smirked because no matter what these niggas were always in sync with me. We all hopped out the car at the same time and I shook my head at Dinero who already had his burner in hand.

"Nigga put that shit up," Ali groaned

"Nigga I can't shoot nobody fuck I come for?" Dinero asked pulling a blunt from behind his ear and a lighter from his pocket.

"Can I smoke?" Dinero look from the two of us.

"Yeah bitch fire up," Lee said and I had to laugh at my brothers. Despite the shit I was going through them niggas kept me grounded.

"What are you doing here?" Lanya ask walking out the house in an oversized pajama shirt, her hair all over her head and no shoes. I looked from Ali to Dinero, before I pulled my gun and nodded for O to do the same.

"Nigga you don't know shit happened," O said swooping Nya up. I dropped my head looking at her lace panties. "Nigga move."

"Nah, Cario chill out."

"Fuck that Alijandrose this bitch bout to die so move."

"Then kill me Sacario," Lanya says and Ali stands in front of her blocking her. I don't care I didn't want her ass no way, I was bout' to body whoever was in my pussy.

"Nigga I'm not killing my baby sister nigga!" Dinero says and I look at him then her and push past Lee to the house Nya just walked out of.

"No Cario stop," Nya yells jumping on my back. I grab both her hands and toss her to the grass.

"Go head kill this baby but you won't kill no one else's." She took me off guard I looked to the ground watching her hold her stomach and cocked my pistol.

"Bitch you fuckin niggas while you holding my seed!" I asked turning my anger back to her. Ali grabbed me as the lawyer nigga ran out the house picking Nya from the ground like I was afraid to body his ass. Dinero walks over to the lawyer grabbing Nya from his hand.

"Fuck was you thinking?" O asked Nya smacking the back of her head, and the lawyer nigga steps in my brother face.

"No Dinero, he has nothing to do with this." Lanya says defending this nigga, I watch my wife defend another man, and I'm beyond ready to kill her.

"Lanya these men don't scare me." The lawyer nigga say's and Ali started to laugh.

"Nigga we should," Ali and Dinero say in unison.

"Get over here now Nya!"

"No Sacario."

"Man take yo ass to yo husband, before I act a fool." Dinero tells her and she holds onto him tightly.

"He gone hit me!" She cries into his arm.

"Have I ever not had ya back?" Dinero asked her showing her his arm that had her name tattooed on it. My blood was starting to boil.

"Let's go Mrs. Alton." I ordered not giving her a chance to react I just grabbed her up and walked her down to my truck. I opened the door to the back seat. I shoved her in and climbed in behind her.

Lanya was shivering and already crying. I could hear my brothers arguing with lawyer dude from outside and I was trying not to get upset. I reached in my pocket pulled my keys and unlocked my Glove box. I placed my burner inside, and then I turned the car on, blasting the heat.

"Take that shirt off now," I ordered her. Taking my shirt off and handing it to her. I ripped the shirt from her hand rolled the window down and tossed the shirt out. I couldn't help but to glance, at the way my brothers had the nigga hemmed up. I rolled the window back up, my attention back on my wife.

I knew I shouldn't but I smacked her upside her head and then pulled her close, before she could react and put her tongue in my mouth.

"You kiss him?"

She shook her head no, that didn't make shit better. I watched tears flood her face and I pulled her on my lap.

"You love me?"

"You don't love me!"

"That's not what I asked you Nya! I said do you love me?"

"I can't keep living like this Killa, Sacario you cheat and lie so much."

"Lanya that's not what the fuck I asked you, but since you can't answer that tell me this how far along are you?"

"18 weeks" I sucked my teeth, I knew she was pregnant and even after the fight we had at the shop she hadn't killed my seed.

"When the fuck was you gone tell me?"

"Last night when I gave you that eight hundred thousand dollar watch, and six hundred thousand dollar car. Forgive me for thinking I was yo wife."

"Don't run that shit on me, you been fucking that nigga?"

"Nigga you sound dumb," she says rolling her eyes at me.

"So he just waited all these years for you?"

"I waited all these years for yo bitch ass!" She yelled covering her face with her hands in fear that I would hit her.

"I love you babe," I told her pulling her lace panties off. I could smell her vanilla body wash, and wanted to taste her. I tossed her down on the back seat and lifted over her, licking my lips, before I dived in. Her hands rushed to my head, her fingers locked in my curls and I could hear her moaning.

"Daddy!" She whined pushing my head in deeper. Her legs were shaking as I drank her juices quenching my thirst. I sat up slowly pulling her onto my lap pulling my dick from my jogging pants and slid inside of her. I held her waist and pounded inside of her.

"Fuck somebody else you hear me? That's it Nya you understand?" My hand slipped around her neck and I pressed down. "Do you understand me?" I pressed until her almond colored skin turned red and I loosened my grip.

"Do you understand me Lanya?"

"Yes," she cried out dropping her head in my chest and crying. I unloaded marking my pussy like a mad dog.

"The shit you got with him is over, you hear me Nya? No more you and him, have no reason to talk or see each other!"

"You gone kill him?" She asked with the saddest eyes I had ever saw.

"You go near him again and yes I will." I kissed her forehead and handed her panties.

"I'm going to go get ya shit, and theses damn fools. Then we go home and talk."

"Carri no, I'm not ready."

"What you mean you not ready?" I asked looking into her sexy brown eyes.

"I just need time to myself. I will stay in a hotel, whatever I just need time to myself please." She whined.

"Yeah you need to get ya shit together, go home check on our children pack a bag and pick a place."

"A place for what?"

"To visit, you need to relax, and I need to work and I can't have you all over the place." She nodded her head, and I opened the car door and climbed out.

"Yo O go get yo sister shit, Lee let's roll."

"What did you do to her, she wants to be with me and you couldn't stand it."

The lawyer nigga said and I almost fell to the ground.

"Nigga that's my wife!"

"Yo wife was fucking me last night and she sure wasn't thinking about yo uneducated ghetto ass!" I didn't even think I just reacted. Visions of Lanya and this smug nigga fuckin invaded my head, and I was gone kill this nigga.

Ali tried to pull us apart, but he was gone have to blow my brains out. I pounded into the nigga, and I was shocked that he was giving as good as he got.

"Cario please I said I would do right please." Lanya cried, I could feel something tugging on me, but until I heard the gun fired into the air did I allow Ali to pull me off that nigga.

"Dumb ass," Ali said walking over to Lanya who was on the ground, holding herself.

"Bitch nigga," the lawyer nigga said and I laughed.

"Killa go." Dinero ordered, I walked towards my wife that Ali stood up and was rocking. Just as I got to her the nigga charged me knocking both me and Nya onto the ground. Dinero grabbed him, but Nya was already on the ground crying. Vomit covered her face and I was ready to kill.

"Killa go," Dinero yelled. Ali lifted Nya into his arms, he took his shirt wiped her face and placed her in the car.

"Nigga take yo wife home."

"No Ali don't please, Cario you promised," Lanya cried and I nodded for both my brothers to follow.

Chapter 29: Deceit I know her

Kym

The sound of my phone ringing wakes me from my sleep. My head is pounding as I search for the phone to silence it. Finally I grab it look at the time, and realize it's four in the morning. Fuck I think to myself, as I glance over at Twan lying in his boxers rubbing his belly in his sleep.

"Dinero is gone to murder me?" I say out loud, but not really talking to anyone.

"Man fuck that nigga you my fuckin wife" Twan says turning over wrapping his arms around me trying to pull me back down.

"No T I have to go! Dinero is already gone to be beyond pissed." I told Twan and watched as he sucked his teeth and his nose flare like a bull.

"Man you still worried about that nigga Kym, What he got over you? Cause babe if it's the money, me and that nigga Santana making a boat load of that shit in Flint. I got you baby" Twan says standing to his feet.

"No Twan it's not the Money I love—

Before I could finish Twan cut my words short with a fist to my lip. I looked up at Twan placing my hand over my lips as tears poured down my cheek.

"Baby I'm sorry" Twan says rushing to my side. He pulls me from the floor into his arms and I pull away.

"How am I gone to explain this to Dinero?" I say out loud.

"That's what the fuck you worried about?" Twan says pushing me back to the floor and starting to kick me. All I could feel was Twan's foot repeatedly crush my body. I wanted to scream, but my head was spinning.

"Fuck Kym I love you, why don't you see that?" Twan screams as he pounds into me and my eyes get heavy.

. I woke up with Twan smoking a blunt and talking on his phone like I wasn't in the room. My body hurting so bad I could barely get to my feet. I managed to pull myself up and walk over to the bed and laying on it.

"Baby I got to make a run, you gone be good Twan talked to me like he hadn't just whooped my ass.

"I have to get to my son Twan please"

"Ok we go get him and come back here!"

"NO! Twan I wanna go home" I tell him sitting up in the bed. He shook his head and rolled his eyes.

"Alight that's cool I need a favor when you get back to that nigga" Twan says and I look at him with a side eye. Was this nigga serious

"Twan I can't get anymore drugs."

"Drugs bitch. I just needed that little shit u gave me to buy my way in with Santana I have a plenty of drugs," I need a big favor and you gone help me"

"What is it T?" He paced the room a bit then he put his blunt out.

"something else" Twan yelled at me. Then he bent down kissing my face with that look in his eye.

I really didn't want to go home I knew Nero would flip seeing my face, and the fact that I didn't answer his phone calls. What really stressed me was how I was gone to pull off what Twan asked of me. My hands shook the whole entire time I drove around the city. The sun was now starting to set and it would be almost two days since I hadn't been home. My phone hadn't stopped ringing and I couldn't bring myself to answer. I knew what I had to do I rolled my car window down and tossed my phone as I drove. I parked my car 10 blocks from our house popped the trunk. My hands were shaking as I pulled my tire iron and broke out the car window. Could this work I questioned, tossing the tire rod back in the car and starting to walk. I waited till I got to a main street and started to scream for help. No one came to my aid so I just continued to walk home. It took about two hours and I was still worried that Dinero wouldn't buy my bull shit, but I had to try. Soon as I got home I noticed that the drive way was packed with cars. Not just family it was a ton of cars. It was no time to turn back. I walked in the door and fell to the floor. No one was in the living room so I sat on my knees and yelled for Dinero

"O! O where are you" I cried and he walked into the room with his gun drawn.

"Fuck yo ass been he asked, before he seen me sitting on the floor.

"Kym what happened?" TaraTara asked and she rushed to help me up. I pushed her away and ran to Dinero.

"Baby what happened he said handing a man I had never seen his gun! Ali and Sacario walked into the room and their flunky that always rolled his eyes at me.

"Babe help me I cried as he lifted me into his arms.

"where is Sean?" I asked breathless"

"He fine hes in his room sleep what the hell happened?"

"Her" I said looking at Nya. "Her fuckin uncle jacked my car had me beaten and tossed me from a moving car like I was trash."

"Fuck you mean" Nero says and I just start to cry, some from fear that Nero will kill me, mostly that I would get away with it and would have to lie to the man I loved forever. Dinero was great he carried me into our bedroom and undressed me.

"babe how you feeling?" he asked running his hands through my hair and kissing me softly. Dinero was so sweet with me as he undressed me and went into the bathroom and ran me a tub full of bathwater.

"For now on you don't go anywhere alone do you understand!" Dinero yelled and lifted me into the tub. He started to wash my body, and I could feel his hands shake. I never seen Dinero so upset, I looked up touching his arm to see tears in his eyes.

"baby I'm ok"

"I know baby because I'ma take care of it." He said taking me from the tub. Dinero was so soft with me I really felt dirty. I loved Nero how could I do this to him just so he wouldn't find out about my past. Dinero tucked me into bed and went to get Jay Sean to lie next to me.

"Where yo phone? He asked rubbing my leg as he sat beside me.

"Yo O we need to go! Sacario came up stairs yelling"

"It was in my purse, everything was in my car"

"Alright I'ma get Saint to stay here tonight tomorrow—

"Tomorrow Luca will be here and he can stay with her"

"What about Nya?" Dinero asked Sacario and he winked at me and smiled.

"she going out of town get some rest" Sacario told Nero and I sighed, Lanya was so lucky she had it so easy, and she always made it so hard I thought rubbing my sons back as Dinero and Sacario talked. Before I knew it the room was still and my eyes were heavy

Ali

Dinero had called us over to find Kym now we were on a fuckin murder mission. As much as I thought I wanted a wife, not like this. Man between Nya and Kym we had enough Drama.

"So baby sis get to the plane ok?"

"Yeah; her and Lissa on the way to Paris." He told me looking back to the road. We had been sitting in the car outside of the Boss's lounge waiting for everyone to show up . finally I was done waiting and hopped out the car.

"Nigga where you going?" Sacario asked following me.

"Shit nigga inside I'm cold as fuck and ready to get shit started these niggas not ready to talk money we can cut these niggas out" I tell him.

We walk inside and I go behind the bar grab a bottle of 1800 and a glass of sprite. I hand my brother a beer and chill waiting for these slow ass niggas, when the nigga killa phone start to ring.

"Yo who this" Sacario yells in the phone, he nods his head. I watch my brother closely he takes a sip from his beer and sucks his teeth not saying a word. However I can tell something has upset him.

Moments later Dinero walked in the room with a crew behind him. I was unsure of who most of them were only two I was sure of was Luca and Saint. I rubbed my head trying to prepare myself. Everyone took a seat and Dinero took the floor.

"Look its like this my wife hiding something so what I'm not gone do is run through the city killing something, but its time to make noise. I refuse to sit back and let a nigga think he can take my city!" Dinero said and I nodded my head.

"Hiding something, nigga you think she setting you up?" Sacario asked and Dinero raised his brow

"Nigga did I say that bull shit! What I said was she is hiding something about what happened and until I know what I am not about to kill everyone.

"How you know she lying?" Sacario asked pissing Dinero off even further. I looked up and Dinero had his gun in his hand pointing it at Cario.

"Nigga stop twisting my fuckin words" Dinero shouted and Sacario laughed

"Nobody twisting yo fuckin words I'm trying to figure out, what the fuck to do and how to handle shit. Sacario yelled as the door opened and eight guns went

313

into the air. They all pointed at the door and eyed the two niggas that walked in.

"Fuck they doing here I asked Sacario, looking at both of my nephews.

"Sup pops Unk, Unk Deuce said hugging every one as he sat down.

"Nigga that's yo team, this mine." Sacario said looking every one over to see their reaction.

So who we got I asked looking at a room full of niggas with murder in their eyes.

You know the nigga Saint and Luca. Well this Nails only bitch ill enough to be on my team, That nigga Cyclone and the nigga Hercules.. Dinero introduced his crew and I crossed my arms over my chest. Saint and I seemed to be on the same page.

"Look yall crew cool as fuck, but I think Deuce and Jay need to stay with Saint. If anyone gone teach them, its gone be blood."

"All eyes were on me as I dropped a skeleton from the closet. Sacario shot me a look and I rolled my eyes.

"Nigga I damn near raised Saint, nobody better to teach them I said Clearfying.

We all agreed and started the meeting.

Lanya

I had been to Paris, Italy, and a few other places in the last three weeks still nothing was like being with my husband and my son. I could tell Alyssa was passed ready to go home and to be honest so was I . I stared out the window of the plane thinking how I wanted everything to be when I returned home.

"Mommy is daddy gone hear the babies in yo belly like me?" Lyssa asked and I smiled. Not yet we cant tell daddy mommy is having two babies, ok" I tell my daughter rubbing her hair thinking about what I will tell my husband when he finds out that we are having twins. After this I am getting my tubes tied my oldest child is 16 I have no business even doing this shit again. I think to myself as I feel the plain land.

As soon as Alyssa and I get off the plain she tells me how she cant wait to see her grandmother. I know she referring to Doris so I call her and Alyssa and I take a cab to her house.

Her home always smells like sugar and she always tries to feed me maybe that's why I loved going to visit her lately.

"Hey ma" I say kissing Dorris's face.

"Oh girl you having boys look how high yo belly is already." I smiled and sat at the dining room table while alyssa takes off into her own little world.

"How did you know I was having Twins I just found out we haven't even seen the babies yet." I ask her and she kissed my face and slide a huge cinnamon roll in front of me. It was homemade and still hot. I couldn't wait to stuff my face.

"Ma what smell so good" I hear Ali say as he walks into the dining room.

"Oh I see he says kissing my face."

"What yo fat butt eating" he asked pulling from my sticky bun and feeding me a bite and putting the rest in his mouth.

"did you just share food pooh butt" Doris asked and I laughed

"Pooh butt,"

"Man shut up, Nya where my niece and when you get back, my brother know you here?" ali asked still eating my food.

"No we just got home and Lyssa wanted to see her grandma"

"Come here Ali said pulling me out my seat. He walked me up stairs into his old bed room and started to rub my stomach.

"Whats up Lee I asked feeling his lips on my neck. Ali and I had been having close calls lately, but this time felt different as he caressed my belly, I could feel he wanted me to react. I pulled away and started to look around his room. I never knew he was in the Army reserve, wow I thought picking up his medals. I couldn't help but admire Ali even more. As I held the award a sharp pain shot through my body and brought me to my knees

"Nya what is it? whats wrong?" Ali asked trying to pull me back to my feet but the pain was so bad I couldn't stand to be touched.

"Nya I cant help you if you don't tell me Ali said to me, but the tears were falling from my eyes, and I could feel my heart start to race.

"Lee it hurts oh God I want Cario please" I cried and Ali pulled me back in his arms and just held me, "its ok, you ok, Ali whispered and I felt at ease I found myself resting enjoying the way it felt. When he caressed my stomach.

"Fuck is this shit?" Sacario says and I damn near choke on my spit. I know how it looked and I wanted to rush to Sacario and tell him it was not at all what it seemed, but Ali had already copped and attitude.

"Fuck you mean nigga, I was rubbing my nephew! We got problems." Ali said stepping away from me and getting in to Sacario face.

"Nigga who is you checkin?" Sacario says I can tell he is feeling for his gun and my heart starts to race.

"Babe its not like that I—Sacario put his hand in my face and was now in Ali's face. They were eye to eye and I was sure it wasn't gone to end well.

"Nigga I have no problem for you touching my wife's stomach, and you bonding with yo nephew! What I do have a problem with is her ass on yo dick, and yall acting like yall a fuckin couple!" Sacario said looking Ali in his face.

"Disrespectful ass bitch" Sacario says taking two steps back and look at me.

"babe it wasn't like that, and I'm sorry if you feel that way, but I got a cramp" I try to tell him, but he wasn't hearing that.

"Fuck ever Nya save that for one of them dumb ass niggas"

"Nigga you tripping and you fuckin no it" Ali says to Sacario causing him to get even madder. Sacario grabbed me by my arm and pulled me into his chest. "You unhappy with me?" he asked and I looked away. He grabbed my face and slammed me into the wall. "You don't hear me Nya? Are you unhappy with me?"

"No Killa I love you, but you hurting me"

"Nigga she pregnant and you gone beat her ass"

"Nigga stay out my business Sacario tells Ali and I start to cry.

"What is going on up here?" Momma Doris asked and Sacario releases me.

"Hey momma, nothing going on I just came to get my girls." Sacario kissed my lips and smacked my ass go get my baby so we can go.

Daddy Alyssa yelled jumping in Sacario's arms.

"Daddy guess what mommy having two babies I heard they heart beat and Seen the awful tower and Grandma said I can stay with her, and make cookies can I? Alyssa yelled.

"yeah baby you can stay, Sacario said kissing Alyssa and placed her to the floor.

"Lets go Lanya" He ordered and I hugged momma Doris, and Kissed Alyssa. Walking past Ali like we had done something wrong. Ali grabbed my hand pulling me to hug him, and Sacario almost went ape.

"Ali stop!" I ordered

"This nigga trying to get a hot slug!" Sacario said and Ali sucked his teeth.

"Bye sis, go head for my blood brother place a bullet in me" Ali and Sacario squared off and I grabbed Sacario so that he wouldn't do anything crazy. I could see the hate in his eyes and this point I just wanted to get the fuck out the fuckin house.

Chapter 30

Lanya

After Sacario picked me up I won't deny he was beyond pissed, but I didn't care I had been gone damn near a month I missed my baby. All I could think about was lying in his arms and riding his snake. He had stayed in the car, and was pouting. Like a brat, I went upstairs and slipped on one of his long T shirts and a pair of socks and went back to the car. "Baby whats wrong?" I asked opening the passenger door and getting back in the car.

"Nya I'm smoking get out" Sacario yelled putting his blunt out.

I rolled the window down and lie my head on his shoulder refusing to get out.

"Man Nya I really just wanna be alone"

"I been gone three weeks and you still want to be alone?" I asked him tears filled my eyes and I can see he didn't care.

"Yeah Ny, I wanna be alone." I sat up straight in the seat and looked Sacario dead in his eye he was pissed and at this point so was I.

"What did I do Sacario?"

"Nothing Nya you never do anything!" He tells me lighting his blunt back and putting it out.

"Nya please let me smoke."

"Go head fire up" he rolled his eyes like a bitch and pulled his phone looking through it like I wasn't there.

"so that's what we on now?"

"You hate me so much you don't want me around."

"See you always in yo fuckin feelings"

"I'm pregnant Sacario" I remind him pointing at my stomach.

"Naw Nya even when the fuck you not!"

"Ok then that's the way I am Killa love me or leave me." I tell him and he cuts his eyes and starts to laugh. I reached over and pulled him to me.

I love you babe, you love me back?"

"You fuckin no I do, I just hate that you be all over my brothers like you don't belong to me!"

"Is that what the fuck this shit about me and Lee? Really Cario now who sound like the insecure school girl I say trying to sneak a peek at his phone. He catches me looking and turns it around so that I can see he is texting Ali. I took the phone and sat up in the passenger seat as I inched my way to Sacario's lap.

"I don't have any panties on!" I tell him sitting on his lap facing him. He smirked and I kissed my husband butter soft lips.

"Man you know you be having me wrapped around yo fuckin finger."

"Yeah I know inchin his stiffness out his jeans and sliding on top.

"Ouch, I cried a little adjusting my body.

"You good Lee Said you was cramping." I couldn't help but laugh at my damn husband. I had told him same shit and he ignored me but his brother say it and it really happened.

"Yeah I'm good yo dick just big as hell" I tell him wrapping my arms around his neck and folding my head into his shoulder to numb the pain I was feeling. My pussy was dripping wet, and I knew Sacario was putting in work as he gripped my hips and rocked me up and down. I knew he loved every second because he had his head on the head rest and his eyes were closed.

"You good baby?" He asked again and I nodded yes kissing and bitting his neck.

"Damn Baby yo pussy to hot get up, Sacario says and I look at him like he dumb. I slide down all the way on his dick and slow grind him, because I knew that was the best way to bring my man to a nut. Sacario gripped my ass and bit down hard on his bottom lip.

"Yeah like that ma" Sacario say bending to kiss my breast and normally this would be when I would come to a climax. "Cario, oh God Cari I Yelled, I wasn't Cumming, and had never faked it with my husband, but this time the pain was so great I had to at least think I enjoyed it. Sacario kissed my lips and released inside of me.

"ah, ah, ah the hell it burn" I screamed" clawing Sacario as he lifted me off his lap.

"who you fuckin nigga" I yell I say punching him!"

"Chill ma relax Nya" he pushed me down in the seat and reached over me pulling my seatbelt on me. He adjusted his pants then his seat.

"fuck you doing I asked as Sacario started the car.

"Chill ma ma, please baby" He begged looking behind him and pulling out the dimly lit driveway. It was then I looked down at his jeans. They were covered in blood. His hands and shirt both had, blood on them, and my vagina was pounding like he was still inside of me. I was afraid to look down. I just ran my hand over my stomach. I didn't even realize Cario's hand was already resting there.

"God please don't take my babies" I cried outloud.

"You alright ma ma, you hear me Nya baby we good Cario said moving his hand from my belly and into my seat. He grabbed his phone and started to dial.

"Yo Lee"

"This is Tara"

"Tara let me speak to my brother" Sacario yelled in to his phone.

He sleep"

"Man bitch give my brother the fuckin phone"

Sacario yelled and I knew he was ready to kill. He didn't wait for Ali to get on the phone he tossed his phone to the floor and drove faster.

"You good ma?" Sacario asked looked from me to the road back to the road. I didn't wanna tell him I was in so much pain I could barley breath. Sacario looked at me and placed his hand on my stomach as we stopped at a red light.

"You Ok?" He asked again and I parted my lips to say yes when the words wouldn't come out. All I could do is scream as I watched a black expidtion come towards us.

Chapter 31

Sacario

I woke up dazed. The air bag dust still burned my eyes and I hear the sirens in the background. Looking over to see my wife is not in the car with me. My heart damn near stopped as I see a man standing outside of the Black Expedition that just crashed into us. He has his phone to his ear and he's pacing between my car and his.

I tried pulling the door open but I had no luck so I leaned over in the passagener seat and kicked the door open. I hopped out looking at the man leaned over Nya . He is holding his arm and has his phone propped on his neck.

"No I don't think shes breathing" the man says and I flip. I look down at my wife and tears flood my face and I charge the nigga like a bull.

"Bitch she was pregnant" I yell pounding my fist into his face. I brought him to the ground and continued to punch him until someone began to pull us apart.

Blood covered my hands and face from where I punched the niggas face in.

"get off me, save my fuckin wife I yell." Pulling away from the hoe ass cops and running to Nya. The EMT is working on her and all I could do is watch in fear.

"She pregnant, wit twins" I say falling to the ground, wondering what I did to deserve the pain of losing my family.

≈≈≈≈≈≈≈

I paced the ER not knowing what the hell was going on.

"Oh my God Sacario, how is she Tara crys running to my arms and I drop my head. Ali is behind me, and he pushes pass her and just hugs me.

"Nigga that's my heart" I say crying on my brother shoulder.

"Yo where she at?" Dinero yell walking in.

"the fuck happened" Dinero asked and I look at him and he falls backwards in the chair.

"she dead?" He ask and I cant even think.

"She was breathing, and she been in surgery three hours.

"Nigga three hours and you, just fuckin calling me" Dinero yells like I had to keep him in the loop on my wife.

"Nigga I got hit too I had to be checked out then I had to wait till they found my fuckin phone I yelled at my brother.

Ali grabbed me and sat me down.

"Alton family?" a slender man of Asian descent walked out and asked.

"Yeah that's us" I answered holding my stomach.

"Ms.—

"Mrs. That's my fuckin wife I correct him"

"I apologize Mrs. Alton has lost a lot of blood. I'm afraid that we had to deliver the babies."

"Can I see them I asked" and the doctor looked away.

"I'm sorry sir, she wasn't far enough along, I estmate no more than twenty weeks." The doctor says and I feel like he has ripped my heart out along with everything else.

"How my wife?"

"Shes gone to need blood—

"Take mine I tell him"

"we have to check to see if you are a match."

"I am I have given her blood before. I say ready to give my wife the heart out my chest if it met she would live.

Lanya

I had been home for two weeks and my body still hurt. However it couldn't compare to the pain in my heart from the loss of my babies. Alyssa had been staying with momma Doris on and off, and Deuce was so busy doing his own thing, the only one home with me most times was Jayson. I loved him like he was mine. At times I wished I could tell him that Sacario was his father.

"Ma you ok Jay asked placing another blanket over my legs and lying beside me in the bed. He turned up the TV and pretended to watch, but I could tell he was really looking at me.

"Jay I'm ok"

"I know, I just wanted to watch TV with you"

"Yo babe you up" Sacario yells walking in the room.

"Hey Killa"

"Sup kidd" Sacario says and I can tell it hurts him not to be close to his son.

"Yeah I'm woke" I say turning over not to look at him. Jay stands up kissing my cheek and then leaves the room. I hear Sacario's boots hit the floor. He then climbs in the bed behind me. I feel his cold body touch mine, and I pull away.

"Move Cario"

"Babe I'm cold warm me up!" he pulls me into his arms and he smells like weed and cherry candy. I turn looking in his soft brown eyes, and he kisses my lips. I can taste the flavored cigar on his lip and I wanna melt. Sacario was so sexy, but I knew if he touched me I would forgive him for letting me live and I wasn't ready, too. I know that was selfish, but I felt so empty I didn't know how to react.

"Move Carri I don't wanna"

"Wanna what babe"

"Be touched! I yelled getting out of the bed and slipping on my jogging pants.

"Man Nya where you going" he asked and I roll my eyes walking out of our bedroom and into the second guest room. The other room I had allowed Jayson to make it his own.

Sacario

Nya was pissing me off. I just wanted her to know I loved her, and she had been pushing me away. I followed her into the guest room and slammed the door.

"Now when I'm fuckin another bitch you can't live without me, but now I'm fuckin here and you mad. Kind of bull shit is that? What the fuck you want from me Nya" She stood from the bed and walked in my space.

"Ion want shit from ya as Killa, you wanna be with another bitch go right ahead, I'm sick of not being enough"

"The hell you mean you not enough Nya" I'm here baby I'm trying"

"Nigga I don't want you to try! If you want me you just be here! If you love me its effortless fuck killa! She yells turning her back. I wrap my arms around her waist and bend kissing her neck.

"I know babe I'm sorry"

"she turned facing me kissing my lips"

"Babe I'm so sorry, I know you hate me"

"Why would I hate you?"

I lost our babies, I'm so sorry she crys lying her head on my chest and I caress her back.

"Not yo fought" I assure her, lifting her into my arms. I lie her in the bed and allow her to cry, just as Lanya is letting her guard down, my phone starts to go off and she pulls away.

"Its almost one in the morning Sacario, what bitch is that"

"Man what Nya?" I say she snatchs my phone from my pocket and I snatch it back. She grabs my hand and bites my wrist taking the phone, Nya

"Hum Olivia, see you made me kill mine and bitch cant carry hers"

"Babe its not what you think"

"You told her" Lanya yells and I go to grab my phone and she tosses it at me.

"Go Cario please just go I fuckin hate you"

"Nya, you don't mean that!"

"Hell I don't I hate yo bitch ass just get the fuck out" She screams slamming the door to the bathroom.

I took a deep breath and look at my phone reading the new text I had just recived.

"Look Ma I got a meet up, I'll be back in a hour I love you I say yelling at the closed bathroom door.

"You not gone say bye"

"fuck you" she yelled and I didn't feel like fighting anymore I just walked out the room walked in our room grabbed an extra clip and slipped my boots back on. Grabbed my shit and was out the door.

It was one in the morning, I had no idea why any nigga would wanna meet me, and however anything to get this shit nipped in the butt. I felt necked pulling up at ecstasy without my brothers, but all the shit Dinero was going through with Kym, I knew pulling up at the Mark's brothers bar would just be crazy, so I texted Saint and my nigga Luca to meet me.

Luca was fresh out of the pen so I wasn't sure how quick to the draw he would be, but if shit went down I wanted to be ready. The sound of my phone ringing made me jump out my skin as I looked down to see my wife face. As mad as she had made me before I left I really didn't feel like answering so I hit ignore and reclined my seat back. I lifted my body and pulled my gun from my waist band so that it can rest on my lap. I didn't realize how tired I was until my eye lids started to get heavy. The tap on the window changed that. I rested my gun in my hand as I sat up to see was trying to get my attention.

"Sup doe my nigga" Luca says as I roll the window down, I opened the door and got out hugging my nigga.

"This yo spot?" Luca asked looking at the wack ass bar that was a sad excuse for a night spot.

"Nah nigga my shit jumping right now I tell him rubbing my hands together. It was freezing and I really didn't feel like waiting for this nigga Money.

"Yo who we waiting for Luca ask as Saint walks over to us blowing in his hands to keep them warm.

"That nigga Money" I tell him and Luca took two steps back.

"Nigga that nigga tried to kill you twice and you in bed with him again." Luca asked and he had my ear.

"Yeah nigga the night Silk set you up that was—The sound of gun fire silenced Luca. I pulled my gun and Saint was already firing back. The car sped by and I could only get one round out, I couldn't believe that shit had just went down like that. I sat my gun on the ground to check on Luca when the sound of tires burning brought me back to my feet. Saint stood to fire however it was too late I could feel my body jerk. I tried to keep standing, but my wind had been knocked out and I fell to the ground.

Chapter 32: Well run dry

Lanya

The sound of banging got me and my boys out of bed. They rushed to the door, before I could get down the stairs.

"Sacario who is it I ask my oldest, Jayson grabs me and trys to turn me from looking,

"Ma go upstairs Jay says and I push him back to see a nigga I don't know and Saint pulling my husband into the house.

"What the hell happened?" I asked Saint rushing to Sacario who is not moving at all.

"It was a set up Killa got hit" Saint tells me and I just start to shake.

"Damn it I can see that! Why did you bring him here I ask screaming.

"Deuce call 911" Jay call Dinero" I order my boys and I cant stop the tears as I drop to my knees and hold my husband's hand.

Sacario, on all I love you better not die"

"He was talking in the car he said bring him here! I thought he was fine we all had vest on till he passed out in the car.

"Yeah you idiot hes bleeding" I yell at Saint and he cuts his eyes at me as siresns pull up.

I pray in my head, but I can smell death and I know that it is in this room As they lift Sacario up on the gurney he grabs my hand.

"Yes baby, I'm here" I tell him and he passes out. I hear one of the men yell something, as they rush him out of the house.

Continued in Part 4

Coming Soon from

Anjela Day

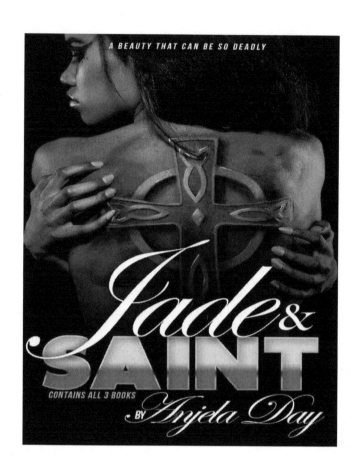

Jade

The beginning

I sat at my mother's vanity she stood behind me brushing my hair. Her hands trembled and tears ran down her face. I had never seen my mother so upset. I wanted to protect her, but I didn't know how or even what to do. I was just a child. She was clearly angry with my father. I had no idea why or what he had done, but whatever he had done left her on edge. She was speaking to me as an adult. Come to think about she spoke to me as if she knew that her time was coming to an end. She leaned down kissing my fore head as the brush strokes my head. I heard her clear her throat.

"Jade I need you to listen to me." She grabbed my chin and turned my face so that we were eye to eye.

"*Jay*" She called me by my nick name,

"One day you're gone to marry your father, and baby that, well that scares me, because your father is not a good man."

My eyes filled with sorrow. *"What was my mother saying? Why would she say that"*

As a child hearing that I was thrilled, on the thought of marrying him! I loved my father. There was no better man to marry; it wasn't until I looked in the mirror with tears running down my face. An empty bed behind me a baby in my belly that I realized I had married my father.

Yeah I was now Mrs. Jade Ashanti Carter. I thought that name would make me happy. After all Sean was the only man that could send chills down my spine. He was also the only man that knew how to keep me in my place. I knew at times I could be a spoiled brat, but Sean. Didn't have that shit. He would hit me with a side eye cross his arms over his chest and I would know that I had over stepped. That I liked about Sean, but it was when Sean became a monster that I knew that I had married my father.   Maybe He had always been a monster, but knowing who Sean was and what he did. Sent chills down my spine in a whole other way. It was easy to overlook it when I didn't know what he was or what he had done, but knowing those nights that he stayed out late it was a 90% chance that someone had lost their life.

I loved my husband. It was nothing that I wouldn't do for him. However, let's face it I was 7 months from becoming a mother, and with a miscarriage and an abortion under my belt I couldn't afford to stay with him.

I looked over at Sean as he dressed, and wanted to beg him to stay home. Standing up from my vanity, I walked behind him wrapping my arms around his waist. He smelt so good. And I wanted him to make love to me. I needed to feel his hard rock inside of me. Running my hands up and down his six-pack had my pussy wet. I couldn't resist planting tiny kisses on his back.

"Um Mami that feel good." He took my hands and pulled me into his arms.

"Why you always fuck me when I get a call and I got to go to work."

"I guess I just be wonting you to give me some."

"Naw baby you know I'm not know fuckin minute man, so that shit not bout to happen, but when I get home...

"When you get home when Sean"

"Not this shit again." He wrapped his arms tighter around me and kissed me sweetly. Taking my tongue in his mouth, and sucked on it.

Um you taste good." Saint spun me around and rested my body against his. He slipped his hands into my panties and ran his middle finger over my clit. I exhaled as he took his other fingers and spread my lips just enough to let two fingers in side of me.

My head fell back on his shoulders and I had to bite my bottom lip so that I wouldn't scream when his fingers went in and out of my pussy. It felt so good I could feel my nipples stiffen and my pussy was so wet I thought that I had peed on him.

"You like that baby?" I nodded my head wishing that he would toss me to the bed the floor I didn't care I just wanted to feel him inside of me. Just the thought of the way he felt mad me moan. Sean kissed my neck running his thumb over my clit faster and faster... I screamed as I could feel myself grinding his fingers, I was ready to cum, and it was no fighting it I took a deep breath as he ran his finger over my clit on last time and I let it go all over his hand. My heart was racing and tears ran down my face. Sean pulled his hand out of my panties and kissed my face.

"I love you Mrs. Carter."

"I love you too" I watched him walk into the bathroom; before I let more tears fall down my face. If I didn't leave to night, I never would. I lay in the bed and pretended to be sleep when Sean walked out the bathroom. He chuckled, and kissed my face. I could hear the front door, close but I couldn't force myself to get out of bed.

Finally after 20 minutes I dragged myself out of bed, showered and grabbed my bags that I had hidden in the back of our closet. I opened the safe and took a few stacks; it was only about two hundred grand. Just until my trust fund kicked in. I sat at my vanity and wrote Sean a letter. Tears flooded my eyes with every word I wrote. I cried so hard just thinking about leaving my husband. I didn't know how I truly would do it. Placing the letter on the bed I grabbed my bag took one last look and walked out of the home I shared with my husband.

Saint

I Love Jay so much that it makes me sick. At times, I feel like she is the only reason I have not went mad. As

345

good as her pussy was feeling this morning I can't wait to dive in. I had been thinking about her juices running down my hand all day, and it's the only reason I rushed up I 96 to get home so quick.

"Jay where you at ma" I yelled walking into her bedroom. It was almost midnight it was odd for her not to be home. I pulled my cell phone and call her phone. Damn voice mail! I walked over to the bed when I see a sheet of paper lying on my pillow.

Sean, I know that I told you I was ready to be your wife. I know I promised to love you know matter what, but it had become clear to me that I can't. I may sound like a coward but baby I swear that is not the case. It's because I love you I know that I can't stay. Every day that We are together I watch you turn into a man that I can't live with, but also hate to be without. I thought I was built for a life style that I had been a part of my whole life, but all that we had been through in the last two years has showed me that I have always been blind to this life. After the death of your brother, and seeing what this game and how this life changes people I can't are to watch us become like those people. No matter how much I love you I now know that THIS WORLD IS NOT FOR ME!

Love Always,

yo wife Jade

Reading this letter has me at a lost. Never have I loved nor trusted a woman and now she has the balls to walks out on me. I never thought that I would regret putting a ring on her finger. I can't dwell on this. I pull out my cell and hit my nigga Psych up.

"Yo nigga lets hit a strip club that bitch left me"

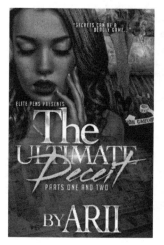 

Coming Soon on

Elite Pens Publishing

look for these titles in digital and print.

F ** K C A N C E R ...

THIS BOOK IS TO ALL WHO HAVE LOST THE FIGHT WITH OR NO SOME ONE THAT HAS I LOVE YOU KEEP YA HEAD UP... I MISS YOU ODESSA DORIS WYNN-BROWN

Acknowledgements

This book is dedicated to my Mother... I love you very much. I hope that you are very proud of the woman you raised. Because I am truly blessed to have the mother I have. You remind me every day that anything that I want is mine with hard work and a Dream... You are my Rock Star mom Happy Birthday... and so many more

Thank God for the so many blessings I have been given... Mainly to tell my story I am truly a blessed person ...

I am very blessed to have very loyal reader's friends and family I thank you all

Thanks for the cover http://www.tspubcreative.com/

And Tyresha for the edits

To My Elite Pen Authors thanks for riding this thing out with me mad Love to our Newbie Mika Melissa and Danny

Allison, Alexzander, Peter, Cre- Cre (my sister) Celia, Lowe (God Mother)

Dorothy Clore... Love you

Alisha Tammy, and Grandma Big huggs

Arabia thanks for always reading and rereading

Carla mad love sis you always look out no matter what

Mad Love to My Twin Arii for always supporting me and loving me no matter what... You my ride & Die chick ... Tasha (Tnicyo) my sissy... thank you for smacking me when needed... Loving me all the time

Gabby Really having my back and reading 1000 and inboxes and keeping it 100 Loves

Stacks you a handful. Jenn You bossy as shit

Owen De'Andre Hayward and AnnJanette

You are my heart beat

India, Shan Ray David Moon and my SBR family thanks for the love and the push to work harder...

556 book chicks and my bestie Tiff thank you for having my back in this industry... yall a-1 happy 1 year and many more

Taya... best friend you read all my books support all my work and listen to all my heart aches you are 1000% in my book ... (my friend) insider

Jane Pennella (my Pooh Face)

Calie Wolf... Love you always auntie

Tammy Jernigan

Charmanie Saquea

Shanicia Jackson

Candy Allen Thanks Tee Tee for every time you read and review my books love you

Wanda Graves you are an awesome woman and I love you ... congrats on reaching your goal as an RN... Bravo

Tenisha Gilbert

Shanicia Jackson

Ollie Moss (my day one)

Shanicia Jackson got u boo

Quiana Brown (wify)

Shikira Hoy your Lol Sis

Janisha Foster

Candace You a boss (heat wave in AK)

Treasure Malian ... Glad you back to team us

Nosha Bawss Peterson

Christine Chrissy J. Joyner

Carl Warts Jr.

Margaret Mccullough

Tiffany Glenn - Miller

Jasmine Shaque' Price & my mommy Andrea Cloud-Williams

Vivian Bailey Urban book lover and Children Books Writer

Angela Corum

LaShawnda Green

Vanessa Speaks

LaLa Williams Me Creola Williams

Jasmine Shaque' Price

Monika Scales-Mitchell 556 book chicks

Nicki Lovingme Williams

If I forgot you please blame my mind not my heart I am truly thankful for each one of you...